The Stainless Steel Sign

Books by Kee Briggs

The Third Removed
The Painted War
Finders-Keepers
Losers-Weepers
The Painted Lady
A Few Good Old Men

The Usher Orlop Mysteries

The Golden Janus /The Pewter Masks
The Nickel Trophy/The Bronze Bones
The Brass Portraits/The Zinc Ormolu
The Silver Scepter/The Rhodium Dragon
The Copper Shakes

Sage Grayling Mysteries

The Yellow Ochre Stain

The Lamp Black Pit

The Cad Red Dot

The Asti Fantasies

Charm Catcher/Dream Weaver

Ebook

Write to Live Longer
The Oregon Vortex - Kindle

The Stainless Steel Sign

Kee Briggs

Keescapes Publishing
Satellite Beach, Florida

The Stainless Steel Sign

Keescapes Publishing books may be ordered through booksellers, Amazon or by contacting:
Keescapes Publishing
90 Flamingo Dr.
Satellite Beach, Florida 32937
www.keescapes.com
KeescapesPublishing@gmail.com

This is a work of fiction. All characters, names, incidents, organizations are all figments of the author's imagination and are used fictionally.

ISBN 978-0-9847524-0-9

The Stainless Steel Sign

Kee Briggs

CHAPTER 1

As Usher waited for his client to make his way to the phone, Usher looked down his calendar. He grimaced a bit as he confirmed what he already knew. There were no new appointments to make any life masks, which were his meal ticket. His attention snapped back to the phone when he heard the receiver being picked up.

"Mr. Orlop."

"Good morning, Mr. Jangala. I'm calling to let you know that I'll be shipping your new piece of sculpture this afternoon."

"Mr. Orlop, could you deliver it in person? I have something I'd like to discuss with you. If you could stay a couple/three days, it would be appreciated. I will pick up your expenses plus time. This is a new subject and it has nothing to do with the boys."

"Just a moment, let me check my calendar." Usher again ran his eyes over the empty page. "I have nothing pressing at the moment. Would tomorrow afternoon be convenient?"

"Yes."

"I'll call if I can't get myself and the sculpture out of here on the same day."

"Thank you, Mr. Orlop." The client hung up.

Usher sat at his desk for a bit of speculation on what could be so important that Jangala would go to all of that added expense. Finally, he shrugged, thinking that rich guys maybe don't consider that small an item as being an expense. He pulled his Rolodex over to get the number for the airfreight company.

It took a while to get things arranged so that both he and his sculpture would fly from Denver to Portland, Oregon, arriving about the same time the next day.

Now he needed to talk with his first floor tenant, Anasette, to see if she would drive him to the airport in the van. The sculpture crate was too large for his classic Shelby Mustang. If Anasette wanted to use the van while he was gone, she'd agree.Usher had strained his finances to buy a commercial brick building in an old part of downtown Denver where the ancient structures were slowly giving away to new, modern edifices that were to be lasting tributes to the architects who designed them. His building ran east and west, from the street to an alley. There was a high, full basement with two floors above ground. Two storefronts faced the street on the east. The south side was use by Usher's sole tenant, Anasette, a petit, former classic dancer, turned jeweler. Behind the storefront was Anasette's studio and living quarters that ran through to the alley. The second storefront was decorated, but vacant. Behind it was a vast storage area and then room for a three-car parking area. Along the alley was the back of Anasette's bedroom, a loading dock and driveway into the interior garage area.

Off the loading dock was a freight elevator, which serviced all three floors. The basement was a sculptor's dream....the wonder studio. The first part was a general work area, which was used mostly for his clay modeling, with its requisite clay bin and modeling stands. The rest of the studio running toward the front was a series of glassed-in rooms to handle drafting, painting, welding, wood work and numerous other activities. Beyond the rooms was storage.

The second floor was Usher's gallery and pad. The front 80 feet was his private show gallery. Behind it was a gourmet kitchen on the north wall and the formal dining area along the south. Next was the mammoth freight elevator in the center of the space. Beyond that was Usher's private area. Against the elevator wall was an enormous custom bed. The rest of the space contained closets, storage, bath and laundry facilities, work desk and computer equipment. There was also a library area with bookshelves, easy chairs, TV and a grand view of the Rockies through custom-made thermo panes that started four feet up and rose to the ceiling.

As Usher passed by the kitchen, he checked the refrigerator to see what was available for lunch. He took the elevator to the first floor, where he knocked on Anasette's door, He hoped he was not interrupting a great creative moment. If so, he'd pay for it later.

When Anasette opened the door, there was a smile on her face, indicating the visit had not created a problem. The petit jeweler was in her winter garb—a floor length, heavy, white terry cloth robe. The toes of gray woolen boot socks peeked out from beneath.

Anasette stepped aside for Usher to quickly enter so as not to lose too much of the warm air.

"How come you're socializing in the middle the day?" said Anasette.

"I thought I'd invite you up for some basil/tomato bisque and a grilled salami sandwich so I can tell you about my call to Jangala."

"Good. I need to get away from polishing." She held up her blackened hands. "Give me 20 minutes."

Usher heard the shower water go on as he ladled soup into the bowls for the microwave. By the time the elevator started down, the aroma of basil and salami offered their own greetings.

Anasette was in a fresh robe. Her great mane of jet-black hair flowed out to her shoulder points. As she navigated the path to her usual stool at the dining bar, she threw in a couple of dance steps.

"What did Mr. Jangala have to say?"

"I was calling him to say I'd be shipping the new sculpture this afternoon and he asked me to deliver it personally."

"What? Why?"

"All he said is that he had something he wishes to discuss with me. He did say it had nothing to do with the boys. I had a real start at first. He asked if I could stay for two or three days. He's willing to pick up the extra cost and time."

"That's all he said?"

"Yeah. I've made arrangements to ship both of us off tomorrow morning. I have to use the van. Do you want to take me out to the airport and pick me up so that you can have the van?"

"I suppose so. With all the snow I can't ride my bike, and I have to do some shopping before you get back. Let's eat."

****

At the Portland airport, Usher rented a van but he had to wait for one to be brought in. To pass the time, he called Lyyli, (Looli) a painter friend, who lived on a houseboat on one of the Columbia River sloughs.

"Usher, where are you?"

"I'm at the airport."

"Good! Can you stop by? A shipment of my book just came in. It looks great. I'm so proud."

"Congratulations. I'm anxious to see it. I have to deliver a sculpture to Jangala. I'm waiting for a vehicle at the moment. When it comes, I have to pick up the sculpture at airfreight. I'll stop by before going to Jangala's."

"Great, I'll get the water hot."

That statement usually set off Usher's alarm. Lyyli didn't serve instant coffee, but used an essence that she made by steeping coffee in cold water.

The watch had been on, for as soon as Usher started down the ramp from the high bank to the floating dock, he spotted Lyyli waving enthusiastically from the front deck of her old houseboat. Tied up alongside was Lyyli's Lair, an ancient day fisher decorated in its bright Finnish traditional colors. The Lair stood out against any background.

Lyyli was a well endowed, statuesque blonde with the type of figure that dragged men's stares in her wake.

Usher was the recipient of a big hug when he stepped aboard. He'd never seen her so fired up. It was too cold to sit on the porch, so Lyyli led the way into the tiny eating area. Most of the cramped quarters had been converted into a painting studio.

Lyyli turned away to get the coffee set up, leaving Usher to discover her new book, T*he Making of the Lower Columbia River,* lying beside his coffee mug.

The book was a 6 x 9 trade paperback with one of Lyyli's paintings of the derelict fish cannery that the Jangala family had once owned on the front cover.

"Wow!" said Usher upon "finding" the book. While Lyyli fussed over the coffee, Usher check out the rest of the book.

"This is great," said Usher. "What's the painting on the back cover?"

"The Astoria waterfront. I painted it from the boat."

"How do you plan on marketing it?"

"Over the years, I've built a pretty good trap line along the river. There are galleries, shops, restaurants and tourist spots where I can consign the books. I'll keep a box on the Lair to resupply my outlets.

"Since you're going to see the Little Tyrant, would you take him a copy? I didn't deal too kindly with his family in a number of spots, but it's the truth as far as I can find out."

"Sure, this should be interesting."

"Could you also be my postman for a few other copies?"

"To whom?"

Lyyli shifted a package onto the table. "There are personalized, signed copies for you, Anasette, Britta, Jon, Eric and one each for the four colonels. Each one of you had a vital part in my finally getting this thing finished."

"I'd be honored to be your postman. However, Britta may not let the boys see this quite yet. She hasn't talked with them about the past. Oh, they'll know all in good time. I think it's Britta who is not ready."

CHAPTER 2

It would have been a struggle for one man to get the heavy wooden sculpture crate from the van into the study, but fortunately a gardener was available to be pressed into service.

Finally, the crate sat in the center of Jangala's study. As Usher was using a wrench to detach the box from the base platform, Jangala made his lurching entrance from the rear. He chucked his two canes into an old umbrella stand before easing himself into his ergonomic chair. "Good afternoon, Mr. Orlop."

"I've never felt comfortable with that 'Mr.' part. I still associate it with stern reprimands. Unless, I'm incurring your ire, please call me Usher. However don't expect me to call you anything but Mr. Jangala. The title rests well with you."

With a rare smile, the old patriarch said, "Very well, Usher it shall be."

Usher returned to his task.

With a slight emphasis on the name, Jangala said, "Usher, you are causing a great degree of anxiety for my interior decorator, Ivan. He did this house decades ago, when we were much younger. Since I've known you, each new sculpture has meant Ivan must adjust his initial flawless design. Ivan and I are contemporaries so you must not put too great a strain on him."

When Usher lifted the box off the figure, it was facing the desk, so Jangala received the full impact of abject despair. Usher had left the dolly beneath the crate, so he could slowly turn the figure in a full circle.

"You certainly captured the moment. Ivan must select its positioning with care because we wouldn't want to cast gloom over joyous events. Thank you, Usher."

"Another item of business," said Usher. "A friend, Lyyli, locally known as Lyyli Lynx, wanted me to give you a complimentary copy of her new book. She says that you and your family are prominently noted. She told me she had to deal with you as factually as she could, which was not flattering, part of the time."

"Don't worry, I've seen reports that run the gamut from brown noses to Stephen King type horror story tellers trying to tell the Jangala story."

Usher laid the book on the ornate desk. "Now you wanted to discuss something with me?"

"Yes, sit down. As soon as the coffee is served, I'll tell you a story. In the meantime, on numerous occasions, you've mentioned your associate, Anasette. Just who is she? I don't even know her last name."

Usher laughed, "Anasette is one of the most intriguing creatures of the world. She never uses a second name. Even if you could spell it, you couldn't pronounce it. Anasette is about my age. She was an up-and-coming ballet dancer when some clod dropped her during a leap and she mangled a metatarsal, which required a career change. She is now a very talented jewelry designer. She carries the whole process from concept and design through to the finished product. She is a fascinating, but challenging person to be around."

The coffee arrived. When the server left, Jangala took a deep breath before saying, "No one knows this but me and now you. When I was 14 or maybe 15, my family was on the rise both monetarily and politically. A pretty and very talented young girl came to work in one of our offices. The staff viewed her as a comer in the business, even though she wasn't family.

"That job was very important to her and I took advantage of

her plans for the future and my position as the owner's son. I got her pregnant. As soon as she knew for sure, she quit and disappeared. In those days, it was considered shameful to have an illegitimate child. I later heard she had a girl.

"I was more pleased with the proof of my virility than anything else. Years later, I came across her name again through a birth announcement of a girl born to the daughter of the girl I had knocked up. That would have been my granddaughter.

"As the years went by more daughters were born. I kept track of them by Nexis checks. Now we're in the present. Nexis came up with a hit on Alecia Arnold, who would be my great, great, granddaughter. She is currently in a Monterey, California hospital. She has been declared clinically brain dead but she is in the final term of a pregnancy and the doctors think that the fetus is still viable. They are trying to save the baby. It's making big medical news."

"How did the mother get 'dead'?"

"That's one of the big questions. She was found on the beach in Carmel, California. She was brutally beaten and presumably left for dead. Beachcombers found her."

"Where do I fit in?" said Usher.

"I would like you to go to California and see what you can find out about the attempted murder, check on the mother situation and see if a viable child is produced."

"That sounds more like a job for a detective than a sculptor."

"I do not wish my name to become connected with this inquiry. I don't want a detective to be privy to this information. As you can probably guess, I've investigated you ever since the run-in with my grandson. You seem to have exhibited a knack for this sort of thing."

"What's your interest in this unfortunate affair?"

Jangala shifted his gaze to the ceiling. "Since Jon and Eric have come into my life, they make the days worth living. I've discovered I have the means to do things that I never considered doing before. Oh, I used to hover over my people, protecting them from various hardships, but always with the goal of maintaining a stable workforce. Now that burden has been shifted to my son and he has installed his own administrative style. It is no longer my problem. I guess I have been looking for a reason to get out of bed in the morning. Each day had become a penance to bear.

"There is still some time before the baby comes to term. I would like you to arrange your calendar to include a discreet investigation into this matter. As far as I know, my name will never be linked to this line. I don't wish to interrupt my current order of succession with another contender, but if an unsatisfactory situation develops, maybe I can help.

"Of course I'll pick up the expenses and make it worth your time. Will you do this for me?"

"Yes, I'll do what I can, with the understanding that I am not a trained investigator, I have no medical knowledge and I'm certainly not a lawyer."

"I know. I'm not looking for those types of expertise. I'm seeking good common sense and an acute observer.

"Unless you have other plans, I made reservations for you at the Monaco. If you'll return at two o'clock tomorrow afternoon I will have collected all of the information I have available. You can review the material and if there is nothing more I can provide, you can return home until you feel it is necessary to act."

Staying at the Monaco was living life a little higher in the food chain than Usher was accustomed. That was made evident by the concierge as he surveyed Usher's casual dress and well-traveled canvas bag, but the old boy knew better than to make any fuss, for this ragbag was, after all, an associate of Mr. Jangala.

Not having come prepared for such accommodations, Usher didn't have clothes suitable for fine dining. He opted for a martini at the bar and then passed on to the café area. While lingering over an after dinner coffee, a waiter brought a phone to the table saying that Mr. Jangala was on the line.

"Mr. Jangala?"

"I have been going through Ms. Lynx's book. It is a fine piece of work. Would you try to arrange for Ms. Lynx and Mr. Jones and, of course, yourself to join me for lunch at my home at 12 noon, day after tomorrow? I have something I would like to discuss with them. This is a casual event. That way I can wear a smoking jacket and not have to struggle into a suit. Let me know one way or the other."

"I'll start calling. Lyyli was at her boathouse earlier and she didn't seem to be preparing for a trip. I don't know about Tanner. I presume he is in Tillamook. I'll give you a call."

It didn't take too long for Usher to make arrangements. The pair would meet at Usher's hotel so that they could travel together, thus arriving at the same time.

Mrs. Kalunki apparently had been waiting, because the front door opened as the trio approached. There was a marked difference in the household manager's attitude to him between the present and Usher's first visit. They were now favored with a brief smile.

Mr. Jangala was already seated at his desk. To sidetrack Tanner's propensity to shake hands, Usher said, "You already know Tanner Jones. Let me introduce Miss. Lyyli Lynx, our new author."

"Miss Inoes," said Jangala as he switched to the Finnish pronunciation. "May I commend you on your achievement? I have read everything that has come out concerning the Columbia River community. Your book is the most authoritative account I have yet found."

"Thank you, Mr. Jangala. I'm afraid I didn't deal with you and your family too kindly...."

"No need to apologize, Ms. Lynx," interrupted Mr. Jangala. "You don't know how hard it is to pull off some of those 'sharp' deals. Our family earned most of the bad press that appeared in public records. Those stories that didn't, were even better."

Lyyli grinned broadly. "I know about some of those, but I had no substantiation."

Jangala acknowledged her statement before indicating that the wet bar, which was normally hidden behind hardwood wall panels, was open.

Usher opted for coffee and he was joined by the other two.

"I thought as much," said Jangala as he thumbed buttons on the edge of his desk to close the bar and summon coffee.

Almost instantly the double door to the office opened to admit Mrs. Kalunki pushing a coffee service cart. Once the guests' needs were filled, Jangala turned to Lyyli to speak in some length in Finnish. He listened intently to her reply.

"Now I know the source of your accuracy, Ms. Lynx. You interviewed the old people, many of whom never learned English. Plus your knowledge of the language probably gave you entrée to the others."

Lunch was announced before the small talk ran out. Jangala waited for his guests to head for the dining room. He hauled himself out the back way to reappear at the rear door of the dining room so he only had to navigate a few feet in public. Jangala seated himself at the head of an extraordinarily long table. The foot of the table was covered with what appeared to be drapery material. It was concealing something.

The meal was a superb presentation of poached whole salmon and tossed salad; hot cheese biscuits and butter rounded out the menu.

Again small talk prevailed, except it was directed by Jangala and it was a thinly veiled information-gathering expedition. Since none of the guests had anything that they wished to hide, it became a game of banter and double entendres.

Usher was beginning to wonder as to the reason for the luncheon. After coffee was poured, the server carefully removed the covering at the foot of the table, revealing stacks of cardboard boxes.

When the guests turned back to the host for an explanation, Jangala gave a rare smile and said, "If there is any blame to be meted out it has to go to Usher."

Usher raised eyebrows and said, "Me?"

"Yes. While you were promoting your last cause, you made a new file folder on my computer desktop and entitled it, 'Jangala Story'. Every time I went to the computer I found that alias staring at me. If nothing else, it got me to thinking along many lines. First, the Jangala story was worth telling as a history of the River Finns. Secondly, I was not the one to tell the Jangala story. It would be tainted if viewed from my perspective. Another consideration was that I am too old to start such a project. If the story should be told and I'm too old to be the storyteller, then I must find someone who can do so.

"Ms. Lynx......"

"Lyyli," corrected the bearer of the name.

"When I read your book, Lyyli, I knew I had found the person who can do an impartial job of presenting all sides of the history of the Columbia River Finns. With your heritage, your knowledge of the language and your familiarity with the area, you can do the job.

"Another thought came to me. My wife, Henna, was an inveterate shutterbug. She took pictures of everything. For decades I ignored her proclivity to take snaps of everything and anything. I just paid the bills and wrote it off as a marriage expense.

"When Henna died, I had all those boxes of prints and negatives hauled to the attic. After Usher's little gambit, I had some of the photos brought down. They are on the end of the table. These represent only a small portion of what she did. There are thousands of images. Realize that she was not a professional, but she had an eye for a good picture and she was always buying the latest equipment."

Jangala turned his attention toward Tanner. "Mr. Jones...."

"Tanner," injected the big man.

"Tanner, when I was talking with a little natural history museum curator over on the coast, she said that you had a knack for searching out, analyzing and tabulating things. Working with these photographs will be a monstrous job. Everything has to be identified and categorized.

"I would invite you and Lyyli to take a look at what there is and see if there is material for a definitive inside look at the lower Columbia Finns. Go take a look while I discuss a matter with Usher."

Eagerly, both Lyyli and Tanner moved to the foot of the table.

Turning his dark eyes to the sculptor, Jangala said, "Usher, I would like to establish a relationship with Jon and Eric." Before Usher could say anything, Jangala pressed on. "I have every intention of keeping my commitments not to intrude into their lives. However, the time is flying by all too quickly. I have no wish to impose anything on Britta or the boys. However, I have certain decisions to make and I can't do so without assessing my possibilities."

"All I can do is relay your request on to Britta," said Usher. "I know she has not suppressed any information about the run-in with your grandson, Asto and your end of the family, but too, she has not volunteered information."

"I want to watch them progress. I have played that CD you gave me of them nearly every night."

"I do know that when those two little guys turn their eyes in your direction you will probably feel them."

Jangala gave the hint of a smile. "I await the day."

Usher had known this day would come. Usher had saved Britta and her boys from a murderous attack from Jangala's rogue grandson who had tried to eliminate competition for the family fortune. Britta wasn't sure the boys were ready to face the full story and the other half of the family yet.

Both Jangala and Usher had been keeping an eye on Lyyli and Tanner, who were excitedly showing one another various photos. When they had sampled all of the boxes, they return to their places.

"Well?" said Jangala.

"Marvelous material," said Lyyli . "From what we see here, we could make a pictorial history of the river such as never been seen before."

"My wife snapped a lot of shots but recorded little about them. She kept track of the exposure times and lens openings when a new film came out. However, as soon as she learned its idiosyncrasies, recordkeeping stopped.

"What are you suggesting?" said Tanner.

Jangala leaned back in his chair. He gazed off into the distance giving the appearance that he was looking beyond the walls and the ceiling. "I feel the Finnish people played a significant role in the history of the lower river. After WWII there was a gradual disintegration of the mother group by sons going off to war. Those who returned had seen a broader world outside and many moved on. Others came back with wives. The outer world began imposing its laws and ways of doing things on us, breaking our unity."

Jangala stopped and redirected his dark eyes back on his guests. "Sorry, I seem to wax philosophical at times. I'm offering to pay for you to sort through this mass of photographs and throw away ones of no value and to catalogue the remainder with two ends in mind. The first is to write a comprehensive illustrated history of the River Finns and secondly to prepare them for donation to a university library. My wife would have liked that.

"Before you decide, I would think you should see the magnitude of the job. Once you have made an appraisal, give me a proposal on how you would proceed and what you would charge. Do you wish to proceed further?"

Tanner and Lyyli looked at one another and each nodded.

Jangala took the head bobs as an affirmative answer. "I will have the rest of the material brought to the front parlor for the time being. If we proceed further, other arrangements will have to be made."

"How do we get access to the material?" said an invigorated Lyyli.

"There is always someone on duty here. I'll leave word with the staff to let you in any time."

"When do you want us to start?" said Tanner.

"Whenever it suits you, keeping in mind that time is not something that I have in abundance."

Usher could see that Jangala was beginning to wear down, so as soon as they had finished their coffee, he said that he must confirm his flight since he was returning to Denver early in the morning.

Neither Tanner nor Lyyli had wanted to show their full exuberance over the material that had been presented in front of Jangala. However, once they were in the van, they were ecstatic.

Lyyli said, "I've been pouring over the historical material of the lower river for years. There are all sorts of documents showing fish production, shipping manifests and a few written descriptions...a lot of them in foreign languages. This is a treasure trove."

"These are completely unedited works. Even the ones that show camera movement, underexposure, over exposure, double exposure are still there....with the negatives. Many are still in the processor's envelopes with dates on them."

CHAPTER 3

The flight to Denver was irritating. Usher had planned on revisiting the material that Jangala had given him, but his window seats seemed to be much too small because of the enormous broad-shouldered man who overreached his space. Making things worse, the man kept trying to read what he was looking at. So Usher turned a little sideways and slept.

Anasette didn't care for night driving in the winter, but she was at baggage claim when Usher made it in from the plane. The great down jacket belied the wispy dancer's figure beneath.

Usher had to give a blow-by-blow account of his whole trip. Anasette counted both Tanner and Lyyli as friends, so she wanted to know the full story, complete with personal reactions. She even climbed into the back of the van, to dig Lyyli's books out of Usher's luggage.

Later, over coffee at Usher's dining bar, Anasette examined Lyyli's literary effort and pronounced it great–at least, in the artistic layout sense.

"Have you ever seen these paintings she used on the front and the back covers?" said Anasette.

"No. She considers them to be the best of her serious paintings. She keeps them in an air-conditioned storage locker because it's too humid to keep them aboard the houseboat, and houseboats seem to burn with a certain degree of regularity."

"At the moment, the two paintings are at the Astoria gallery because of the release of the book. Actually, they're not for sale. She's put a ridiculous price on them so no one will be tempted."

"How come you have so many copies of the book?"

"There's one there for you. Each are signed and personalized. There's one for each of the colonels, Britta and the boys."

Anasette looked up sharply. "Are you going to give the boys their copies?"

"No. I'll give them to Britta to use as she sees fit. This may be the vehicle to introduce Jangala. He wants to establish some sort of relationship. He's exhibiting all of the characteristics of a lonely old man. We'll take the books out to the farmhouse while the boys are in school. That way Britta can control the situation."

After Anasette had retired to her apartment, Usher settled down with a brandy to look over the material that Jangala had given him.

There was a sizable stack of paper but most of it was various reporters' impressions of precious few facts. Boiled down, the known facts were that Arnold, age 17 and in the third trimester of pregnancy, was found severely beaten about the head and shoulders on a beach in Carmel, California. She was declared brain dead at the hospital. However, the baby was still alive. Authorities decided to keep the mother's organs functioning in hopes of saving the baby. There were indications that the body had been dragged toward the parking lot, which brought about speculation that the assailant was either trying to take the victim for medical attention or to attempt to dispose of the body. There were no suspects. The soft sand had yielded no usable footprints. There were no known witnesses.

Even though all the reports covered the same material, Usher read each minutely hoping to find some gem left out of the other accounts. Nothing had been said about family. Usher went back to the reports and came up with an out-of-town address, which didn't mean a thing to him. He'd look it up later. What he did glean, was that Alecia lived in one place and went to school elsewhere and that Carmel Beach was a long way out of her normal territory. Usher would have to look closer at that situation. There was no police report included in the bundle, so there was no forensic material available. In a follow-up report there was a description of an old Chevy that was thought to be owned by the victim.

When Usher replenished his brandy, he picked up a road atlas. Arnold's home address was listed as Petaluma, California. She had been going to school at Santa Rosa Junior College, which looked to be about 15 miles north. The attack was in Carmel, which is about 150 miles south. That was a long hike on a weekday. Usher tried to make a list of legitimate reasons for her to go that far on a school night, but without more facts, it was all wild speculation.

When there wasn't any further material to be gleaned from the assault reports, he turned to the accounts of the medical wonders that they were hoping to pull off. Usher wasn't particularly concerned over how they hoped to achieve their goals of getting a viable baby out of the tragic situation. Apparently, this was an accidental pregnancy. No father was ever mentioned.

The murder gained only local attention but the attempt to save the fetus had gotten worldwide publicity. Still no relatives had stepped forward.

The medical staff was not concerned with any delivery date. It really didn't matter. When a problem developed or when the victim decided it was time to enter the world, the doctors would go in and take the baby. Once the baby was born, they expected the mother's systems to just shut down. If not, they were prepared to pull the plug.

Usher revisited his calendar. He didn't want anything important to be in the way when the call came.

CHAPTER 4

The call came in the middle of the night from Jangala. His Nexis search had alerted him to the impending birth. The mother's body was showing signs of labor. The doctors were watching the involuntary reactions of the mother. The notoriety of the case had created a frenzy of activity in both the medical profession and the media. A decision was made to transfer the mother's body and child to the San Jose Regional Medical Center where there was a large surgical amphitheater so more could watch the delivery.

Jangala was angered that such a tragedy should become a media circus. His final instructions were to find out what was happening. Use any means available.

It was still the tail end of the holiday season. Usher had trouble getting a flight. Hardening economic times had forced the strapped airlines to reduce the number of flights, and there was substantial overbooking. The next available flight was a redeye for the next night. Since he had the whole day, he called Kaz Szedlak, a lieutenant on the Denver Police Department.

"Hi Kaz, this is Usher Orlop."

"What do you want?"

"What makes you think I want something?" said Usher in his "hurt" voice.

"That's the only time I hear from you."

"Don't those victory celebrations with prime rib, or whatever, count?"

"You do lay out a good feed," allowed the lieutenant. "What do you want?"

"Tomorrow night I'm leaving for California for a time, but before I go, I thought you might enjoy noodling a case I'll be bumping into down there. I'm buying the coffee."

"Unless something comes up, I'll drop by."

Anasette would let the lieutenant in. She wasn't about to miss a moment of their conversation. When Szedlak arrived the two men shook hands. Usher was very protective of his hands, so letting Szedlak take his hand was a pretty big leap of faith. Szedlak was built like a linebacker for the Denver Broncos. He could crush the sculptor's hand if he set his mind to it. However, over time a substantial mutual respect had built up between them, so Usher had no qualms over a handshake.

After coffee was poured, they took up their usual positions around the counter, with Anasette in the middle. The lieutenant said, "What's this case you may 'bump into'?"

"I have a client who thinks that there is a chance that a murder victim is a shirttail relative. He wants me make a few discrete inquiries and find out what's happening."

Usher laid out the case, indicating that his interest was in seeing to the welfare of the child instead of worrying about the murder.

He got a baleful look from both Szedlak and Anasette.

As Szedlak started browsing through the files, he said, "There is no police report here."

"My client's an old man. He probably didn't have the clout to get one."

"You can't noodle a thing without information. Hand me the phone."

While the lieutenant was spreading a line of crap to get his office to request a police report from Carmel, Anasette was grinning at Usher behind the lieutenant's back.

"We can't even speculate on the act of dragging of the body toward the parking lot until we know what other destinations the killer rejected."

Szedlak glanced at the news reports and Usher's files. "There's nothing here that's useful. Hope the Carmel PD is a professional outfit. I've got to get to the office. When the report comes in I'll bring it over. No need to come down, I can let myself out."

After the lieutenant left, Anasette said, "What do you think Jangala will do, if he gets a live baby? I would think there is a very high chance of getting less than a perfect child."

"I imagine he's thought about it, but if he's made a decision he hasn't confided in me."

Since he didn't want to leave his Shelby Mustang to the winter ravages of long-term parking, Anasette took him to the airport again. In San Francisco he rented a nondescript medium-sized car. Due to the hour, he checked into a motel with an adequate bar and dining room, where he scanned all the local newspapers over a martini. As of press time, the world was still waiting.

Before going to his room, Usher stopped by the lobby where WiFi was available and downloaded Szedlak's contribution-the Carmel police report.

The report consisted of a rant from Szedlak. His request had been returned with a vague statement that the initial crime reports are currently unavailable due to a computer malfunction. Usher could visualize Szedlak's reaction.

Without a police report to review, Usher had to content himself with reading the archival files of the various regional newspapers. The TV websites offered a grain or two of additional information.

Before it was too late, Usher called Jangala to tell him about the problems with the police report. He asked if Jangala had any strings he could pull to see what was wrong.

"That's outside my realm of influence. I don't want to do anything that can connect my name with this case. You'll just have to be inventive."

"Do you know where Alecia was born?"

"Astoria."

"Does Astoria have its own newspaper?"

"The Daily Astorian."

"Thanks. I'll get back to you as soon as I have anything to report."

****

Usher had to jump out of the shower to listen to a TV news item, which stated that various participating authorities were going to give a press conference at 10 am in front of the Santa Rosa Regional Medical Center to let the public know what would happen in the Arnold case.

Dripping his way back to the bathroom, Usher completed his morning ablutions. Before going out for breakfast, he downloaded a Google map of the medical center.

Usher left himself plenty of lead time to get to the news conference, which proved fortunate. It wasn't where he assumed it to be. He had to drive around before he spotted the towers on the TV trucks.

A sizable crowd had assembled in front of one of the large buildings. It was an outside standup event that was open to the public. Usher took note of how various media types were displaying their credentials.

After a workman ran some sound checks on the PA system mounted on the lectern, four men advanced to the microphones.

One of the suits started out the event by introducing himself and stating he was the director of the San Jose Regional Medical Center. He welcomed everybody and launched himself into his remarks.

"Arnold has been moved from Monterey to this facility because we have an advanced maternity facility with sufficient space to accommodate the impending delivery. We don't know when that will be. The medical staff will speak to that shortly. At the moment, a judge is hearing arguments on a request to make Arnold a ward of the court. To date, no next of kin has stepped forward and she is a minor. Her birth certificate lists no father, and the mother has dropped out of sight. We can't proceed until Arnold's legal status has been established.

"Now let me turn the mike over to Dr. Bristol McCann to explain the medical side of the situation."

The man in the white smock stepped forward. After spelling his full name for the reporters, Dr. McCann presented his material. "Everyone knows that Arnold has been declared brain dead. The body has been functioning for the sole purpose of trying to save her daughter. We believe the fetus is near full term.

"When Arnold becomes a ward of the court, her case history will be presented and the medical authorities will recommend the baby be taken by cesarean section. Following the delivery of the baby, Arnold will be removed from the machines, which will result in total death. Further plans cannot be made until legal matters are settled, unless the baby decides to enter the world on its own.

"Now the Carmel Police and the Monterey Sheriff's office wish to have a word."

The doctor stepped back to let the uniformed officer take the lectern.

"My name is Ron Davis, chief of CPD. Since the body was found in our jurisdiction, we are the lead investigators. However, the Monterey Sheriff's office has bigger forensic capabilities, so we are working the case jointly. We are here today to make a plea to the public for information, which is sorely needed in this case. We have a name, address and school of a pregnant minor who was living on her own, supporting herself and attending college. No next of kin has shown up, none of her associates know anything about her. If anyone has any information concerning Arnold we would certainly appreciate your help."

Usher's concentration was shattered by a familiar voice behind him saying, "Well, if it isn't our well-traveled ghoul sculptor just waiting for another poor soul to die."

Standing just behind Usher's left shoulder was Kalib Kahn, a staff reporter for the sensationalist tabloid, "The Orbiter." He and Usher were similar in many physical ways such as age, height, weight and hair color, but that is where all likeness stopped. Kahn had gained substantial notoriety in the field of yellow journalism. He had a real talent for putting the vilest twist on any action or thought his target could have. He was an inveterate liar and he would go to any lengths to get a story, which he would always make juicier.

Usher had crossed paths with Kahn on several occasions. On their first encounter, Kahn had come away with both eyebrows split open. Keloidal scars had left vivid purple ridges that resembled hair trying to grow around a strip of rope.

Kahn was the last person in the world that Usher wanted to connect him with Arnold. His mind was racing, trying to come up with an excuse for being at the news conference. He decided that any reason he might offer would either be immediately rejected or ignored, so he decided not to try.

"Well, if it isn't Mr. Kalib Kahn in the flesh." Usher's eyes switched to the scars....a motion that was not missed.

Kahn's hands involuntarily went to his forehead. "You bastard," he snarled. "I'm going to get you back."

Kahn was getting red in the face. He opened his mouth to say something but nothing came out. He whipped around and tromped back toward the parking lot.

As Usher watched the departing figure, he knew that the confrontation was not over. Kahn would just go into sly mode. Kahn wouldn't stand in front of him. That was not his modus operandi. He preferred to work in the shadows.

Usher's consideration of his new problem was interrupted by the general exodus of the reporters and crews. The news conference had ended. He hoped he hadn't missed anything important.

After Usher retrieved his rental car, he pulled into the first big-box store to buy a prepaid cell phone. With Kalib Khan on the scene, he didn't want his regular cell phone to establish a connection with Jangala. He didn't know how much clout "The Orbiter" had to get phone records. He wouldn't take any chances.

Usher headed straight back for his motel. There were several jobs ahead of him. Concentrating on other matters, he almost missed seeing Kalib Khan pull in front of him to get into the Holiday Inn. Usher was positive that Khan had not seen him. The reporter was driving a nondescript tan Ford sedan. Usher was able to pick up the last three numbers on the license plate.

Although he was tempted to see if Khan was staying there or if he was working a story, caution won out over curiosity.

While waiting for the phone battery to charge, Usher headed for the restaurant for lunch. Being the off-season, there were a few people eating. He had his pick of tables. He chose one by the window next to the pool.

After the waitress left, Usher began making a list of supplies he needed. Out of his peripheral vision he noticed a figure outside the window momentarily hesitate. By the time he looked up, all he could see was the rear view of a well turned blonde woman walking briskly away. Since Usher sighted nothing familiar, he returned to his list.

"Are you a friend of that snake, Kalib Khan?" said a forceful female voice from over Usher's left shoulder. It was the poolside blonde, who would have looked even better from the front if she hadn't been frowning so fiercely.

"I know him, but I wouldn't say that we were friends."

"Do you know why he's here?"

Usher shrugged, "I have no idea, other than he was at the Arnold news conference. That seems to be a subject he would find interesting."

"Then you're not from 'The Orbiter'?"

"No, I'm not from 'The Orbiter'."

"I'm sorry. He's my cousin and he is the black sheep of the family....always making trouble for us and it looks like he's going to do it again."

The blonde was standing up against the booth so Usher couldn't stand. "Why don't you sit down before I get a kink in my neck?"

"Oh, I'm sorry." As she slid into the seat across from him, Usher was taking inventory. She was about his age and well put together. Her features were defined without being harsh. From the way she was turned out, Usher wondered if she was a clothes horse.

"I'm Usher Orlop." Usher raised his eyebrows as if expecting a similar offering in return. Instead he was rewarded with unbridled cheer-bearing laughter.

Usher was beginning to get miffed as she struggled to regain control.

"I'm sorry, but you're the one who gave Kalib his eyebrows. That was one of the greatest gifts anyone could have given this country. Kalib was always changing his appearance when he was digging up dirt on people. Now with those eyebrows he has to stay Kalib Khan or at least only one person.

"I'm sorry but when you turned out to be the eyebrow guy and I thought you were working in cahoots with him, it just struck me as being hilarious."

"Do you have a name?"

"I'm sorry. I'm Sasha Khan."

"Hi, Sasha. I gather that you don't get along well with your cousin."

"No one in the family does. Everyone is prey to Kalib, especially his own family."

"How does his presence here constitute a threat to you?"

"I'm a medical illustrator. I've been hired by Dr. Bristol McCann, the principal obstetrician on this case, to provide drawings of all interesting developments. This case has attracted international attention. It is a pathetic enough situation, without Kalib turning it into a horror show and contaminating everyone involved."

"Watch out, you'll pick up the label of ghoul illustrator."

"That's right, you are the ghoul sculptor." Sasha's laughter quickly faded. "It's even worse because I'm expecting a marriage proposal from Dr. McCann. The family knows we've been getting serious so I expect Kalib knows too. He would like nothing better than to screw things up."

"Now we can be a trio, ghoul sculptor, ghoul illustrator and ghoul obstetrician."

"Oh, quit," said Sasha with too much force. Heads turned. "I'm sorry. I didn't mean to draw attention to us."

"Will you quit apologizing for Kalib and everything else?"

"I'm sorry, this...." Sasha stopped speaking as she caught Usher's expression. She gave Usher a smile before continuing. "This whole affair with Kalib has rattled my cage."

"What's Kalib done with his eyebrows? They look different."

"If he had surgery to remove that keloidal tissue, he'd have lost his eyebrows completely and he still would look strange. He had that purple skin that pooches through tattooed. Now he looks as if he has big, bushy eyebrows."

"I guess it's a small improvement."

"Why are you here?" said Sasha.

"I'm just doing a favor for a friend. This friend asked me to keep track of what was going on. I have no personal interest in the matter."

"I'm content with that explanation, but I doubt if my cousin will accept it."

"He may be curious, but he probably won't do anything personally. The last time I came to his attention, he passed it off to someone else."

"How did you manage that? He has a real thing for you."

"He doesn't like how I react to harassment. Do you live around here?"

"No, I actually live on the beach at Half Moon Bay. Until this Arnold case is over, I'm staying here at the motel."

Usher gave her a quizzical look.

"I'm sor...."

Usher wrapped his mug on a tabletop.

Sasha's ears turned red. Usher didn't know if the new color came from getting caught in her speech pattern or the love relationship.

Further conversation was cut off by the waitress finally showing up to ask Sasha if she wanted to order.

"Just unsweetened iced tea."

When Sasha turned back to Usher she was perfectly composed again. "Bristol and I are playing it very straight with so much attention focused on the college and the medical staff in particular. Normally, I wouldn't be staying at the motel." She punctured the statement with a smirk.

Usher acknowledged the arrangement before turning to the business at hand. "What can we expect from here on out?"

"When the doctors decide it is time to take the baby, Alecia will be moved into the operating theater. This is a dinosaur left over from an earlier time. Modern features have been added. It was rather like an elevated theater in the round where one looks down on the procedure. The mirrors hanging down from the ceiling have been replaced with flat screen TVs hooked up to various cameras. The whole thing will be recorded."

"Who gets admitted to the event?" said Usher.

"Mostly interested medical groups, or institutions can have representatives. This is taken on the air of a fundraiser for the medical center so all the TV networks and cable channels and newspapers will be there. A fund raising plea will probably be attached."

Usher's food and Sasha's tea arrived at the same time.

"As I recall, you are a sculptor," said Sasha after a sip of tea. "What kind of sculptor are you?"

"I do figurative work in bronze and my day-by-day meal ticket is making life masks of people, usually children, that are translated into silver masks.

"But not here...."

"I'm from Denver but I travel all over the country doing the masks. I've never had a show in California."

"I'd like to see your work."

Usher fished a business card from his billfold and handed to Sasha. "Go to my website. You'll see a representative sample.

"Are you one of the new, modern computer illustrators?"

"No, I still do things by hand, the old-fashioned way, to show a point, not to sell a product. I try to stay on the scientific side instead of the advertising side."

Sasha finished her tea. "I must run. I'm to meet Bristol to go over some layouts that need illustrations. It's been neat meeting the one responsible for those eyebrows. The rest of the family will have a good laugh."

Usher didn't dally over the rest of his meal. There was much to do. When he returned to his room, he had enough of a charge in the cell phone to register it and get a number.

Anasette answered her phone, indicating she was not lost in a creative fog. If that were the case, she might not answer her phone or check her answering service for days.

"The baby hasn't arrived yet. We're still in a waiting mode but things have gotten interesting."

"What are you up to now?" said Anasette.

"I ran into our old friend, Kalib Khan."

"Although I hadn't thought of it, that doesn't surprise me. That's the kind of story he thrives on. Did he see you?"

"Yep, he spotted me first. He's curious about why I'm here."

"There will probably be another ghoul story."

"The most interesting part of that meeting was that I was observed by Kahn's cousin."

Usher proceeded to tell Anasette about the meeting with Sasha.

"Since Kahn is on the scene," said Usher, "I don't want to leave any trail between me and Jangala. I bought a prepaid cell phone. Would you call Jangala and give him a new number so that he can answer my calls?" Usher gave Anasette the number.

"Has Szedlak sent you a police report?" said Anasette.

"He emailed me that there had been a computer problem and none was available. I haven't checked into that yet, but something sounds fishy. I'm playing everything moment by moment. That baby has a lot of people sitting around."

When Usher got off the phone, he started working on his computer. He called up the "Daily Astorian" on the Internet and copied their masthead. Transferring the masthead to Photoshop, he fabricated an ID badge with his name on it. Using the three-in-one cheap printer he'd picked up while buying the phone, he printed an ID badge. To complete the job, he ran out to an office supply to get an ID badge holder and a brightly colored neckband.

Before heading back to the motel, he cruised through the Holiday Inn. Usher spotted a car of the same type and color he'd seen Kahn driving. Since he didn't want Kahn to spot him snooping around, Usher returned to his hotel to watch the news.

Usher's phone was blinking, indicating there was a message. It turned out to be Sasha.

When Usher returned her call, Sasha said, "Hi, I have some

information I'll pass on to you."

"Good, but can I buy you a drink? It's about my martini time."

"Give me 10 minutes and I'll meet you in the bar." Fifteen minutes later, Sasha came rushing in saying "I'm sorry, I...." Usher gave her a baleful look.

Sasha rolled her eyes and started again "Just after I hung up, Bristol called me to elaborate on the email I'd received. All authorized spectators had to give their e-mail address so they could be notified.

"All the paperwork is in. Both the mother and the baby are wards of the state. One of the nurses is the guardian ad litem. If there is a viable baby, other arrangements will be made.

"The powers-to-be have decided to take the baby at 7:00 in the morning. There will be no public announcement; they're trying to limit the number of spectators who will try to get in." There was a pause to give the hostess their orders.

"Are they going to be checking names?"

"I don't know. Meet me outside the theater at 6:50. Everyone knows me. We'll walk in together." Sasha snickered. "I can't wait to see Kalib's face when we show up together.

"Oh, yes, I went to your website. I liked what I saw. Why don't you bring a sketchbook? If nothing else, I'll take you in as my assistant."

"Thanks. I appreciate that. Are you going to hang around after the birth or go home?"

"I have no idea. Bristol and I will review the films and decide what to illustrate. Much depends on the condition of the baby. If there are deformities or defects in her, then there will be a lot of drawings. If she is a normal, healthy baby, then there won't be much work."

"I would hate to see you lose work, but I hope the little gal is perfect. She already has a couple of strikes against her."

"I'm with you on that."

CHAPTER 5

Usher located the hall early. He waited in his car in the parking lot to see who might show up. He immediately noticed that he was not alone. Another car, which look suspiciously like an unmarked police car, contained two men watching the earlier arrivals and the building too.

At 6:50 Sasha's car darted into the lot. She was running late again. Usher, with a sketchbook under his arm, set an intercept course to join up with Sasha.

"Oh, I'm....late again."

Usher smiled a greeting and an acknowledgment of Sasha's mental nimbleness. "It appears there is still ample attendance."

"Did you see Kalib?"

"If he's still driving the same car, he didn't arrive before me. As the lot began to fill I couldn't see all the cars."

"Actually, if he parked in the public lot, it would be out of character. He'd be more inclined to sneak into the staff parking, hoping a couple of faculty members will show some little innocuous intimacy that he can twist into a disgusting feature article."

As he passed the suspected unmarked police car, Usher smiled at the two occupants and nodded a greeting. He was rewarded with sour looks before both men discovered an item of interest in the opposite direction.

Inside the front door, Usher slipped the gaudy tape with its ID over his head. They used the stairs instead of joining the crowd waiting at the elevator. There was a set of double doors open with an attendant on each side. Some people were entering unchallenged, while others were being questioned.

"I don't know either of those guys. Let's go around to the other side. There's another door over there. We'll try it."

There were fewer people on the far side. Sasha opened her sketchbook and started explaining a complex medical concept. As they reached the door, Sasha looked up, smiled brightly and said, "Hi, Josh." She walked right by him with Usher in tow as she continued to explain her sketch.

"Josh is one of the interns. He works with Bristol. We'll have the best view over to the left. We'll be closer to the screen showing the most.

The room had been completely altered. Usher could only guess what the tiered seating had looked like. The floor window was solid tile. Now, flat screen TVs lined one wall with seats, comfortable enough for the long haul, lined up in front. Most of the seats were full.

Sasha opted to stand along the left wall. "Dr. McCann has a tendency to hover. The left camera gets the best view."

Alecia was already on the operating table, fully covered with green fabric. The various support people were moving into positions. When all was set, Dr. McCann stepped into view. A nurse folded back a cloth to expose the necessary skin area. The doctor stuck out a hand to receive an instrument. It seemed to take only a moment before he was manipulating a loudly squalling infant. As soon as the umbilical cord was attended to, McCann held up the baby, faced the main camera and said "We have a perfectly formed baby girl," as he held the infant for the gallery to see.

As a cheer went up from the spectators, Usher took the opportunity to search for Kahn. Fortunately, he looked to the rear door first. Kahn was just pulling back, but Usher spotted him.

"Your cousin just left by the back door."

Sasha grinned. "Did he see us?"

"Oh, I'm sure he did. He's a very astute observer."

When Usher turned back, Alecia was already covered. A nurse was carrying a bundled baby away. Dr. McCann stepped to the console where he threw a switch. All machinery stopped working.

Dr. McCann stood in front of the console for a long moment before he turned to face the primary camera to say, "Will the ushers please clear the gallery and secure the doors."

The news people, who had schedules to meet, hustled out. Many of the medical people were clustered together to discuss the situation. The ushers moved into the room to empty the facility.

"What's the rush?" asked Usher.

"The criminal pathologists will conduct an investigation of the beating. Also the organ harvesting will begin immediately. None of that is for public consumption. However, they are going to use this as a training session for advanced students in those fields. They are probably outside waiting."

"When do you start work?"

Sometime this afternoon, I'll probably meet with Bristol. By then, they will have had an opportunity to examine the baby. We already know that there are no surface deficiencies, but there could be a host of problems beneath the skin."

"I don't suppose he'll find anything wrong with her lungs."

Sasha grinned. "I'd guess that you're right."

"It's going to be a while before I can call in my report. How about breakfast back at the motel?"

"Great. I think the buffet is still on."

As Usher headed for his car, he spotted a car parked down the street that could be Kahn's. When Usher pulled onto the street, the car fell in behind. The sculptor debated with himself whether or not he should take Kahn on a scenic tour of San Jose before losing him, or lead him back to the motel. Since he may be checking out to go elsewhere or even home, Usher decided he'd rather have breakfast with Sasha.

His breakfast companion took time to change clothes and attend to her grooming. Usher decided that "delays" would be a built in fact when dealing with Sasha. As he watched her wend her way toward the secluded booth Usher had selected, he decided that the little delay had been worthwhile.

Sasha opened her mouth to speak. She closed it before saying, "I'm getting better." Without sitting down, she said, "I'm starving. Let's go through the line." With heaped plates in front of them Usher asked, "Does Kalib know where you're staying?"

"I don't know, but I rather doubt it. Normally, I wouldn't be of any interest to him."

"He probably knows now. He tailed me from the medical facility. I wouldn't be surprised if he's watching us at the moment."

"That lout! He feeds on the troubles he can cause people. Why is he tailing you?"

"He probably is curious as to why I am here. He is not about to pass up the possibilities that there might be a story here."

By the time Usher finished eating breakfast, it was late enough to call Jangala. The old man must've been waiting for the call, since Mrs. Kalunki handed the receiver to him.

"The news just carried a report that the baby had been born, but not much more."

"Yes, there was 7:00 o'clock call this morning."

"Did you see the delivery?"

"Yes. It was a cesarean section. They were very punctual. Alecia was all prepped. The doctor walked in and, if you had blinked, you would have missed the whole thing. Suddenly, the doctor was holding a very loud little girl. After they dealt with the umbilical cord, the doctor held the baby up to the cameras and said that it appears that we have a physically perfect baby. He handed the infant to a nurse who wrapped it in a covering before leaving the room.

"There was no closure. The doctor, named Bristol McCann, pulled the sheet over the body and stepped to the console to cut off life support."

There was silence on the other side of the line.

"All the spectators were ordered out of the viewing room so the forensic people and the organ harvesters could do their work."

"What is the status of the child?"

"Alecia and the infant were made wards of the court and a nurse was appointed as a guardian ad litem."

"You seem to have better information than the media. How did you manage that?"

"I ran into an old enemy who has a cousin who hates him. The cousin turned out to be the medical illustrator on this case. Also, she is almost engaged to Dr. McCann. I got lucky."

"So the baby is perfect."

"They don't know yet. She is being evaluated now to see if there are any internal problems that are discernible. I think Sasha, the illustrator cousin, should know by tomorrow. She'll probably tell me."

"Has there been any activity on finding the killer?"

"Not that I have heard of. I do know that there is no police report available because of an unexplained computer glitch. I would presume that the responding officers would be rewriting their reports if the first disappeared into the ether. I'd like to see those reports. Several things about this affair bother me."

"Such as?"

"What was Alecia doing on a Carmel beach late at night 150 miles from home? I wonder if she was prepared to spend the night. Without a police report, I don't know if she had overnight luggage in her car or whether she had checked into a motel. No parent has turned up despite a presumed police search and all of the international publicity this case has gotten. I don't know what she was wearing or carrying with her. Was she a victim of robbery? There are all sorts of questions that keep rattling around in my head."

"Stay for a few days to see if you can answer any of those. I would like to know a little more. In the meantime, I'll find some computer files I tucked away somewhere that might shed some light on relatives."

When Usher called Sasha to see if she was available for dinner, he was turned down. She was going over to Dr. McCann's house for a quiet evening.

"I may be here for lunch tomorrow if you're still around. Originally, I planned on returning to the coast after the delivery, but Bristol hasn't made up his mind on the illustrations. Actually,

I think he just wants me to stick around for a little longer."

"It appears I'll be here a little bit longer. Tomorrow afternoon I think I'll take a run down to Carmel-by-the-Sea to look around."

"You said you weren't investigating this case."

"I'm not. I'm just scratching a personal itch. Besides, it's better than sitting around a motel. This is the first time I've been around here. I'm just taking advantage of an opportunity."

The afternoon dragged by. Usher wrote a brief report on the birth. There wasn't much to say. And he started to list all of the inconsistencies that were bothering him. He turned his attention to the TV for the newscast. His store of knowledge wasn't enhanced.

Eventually martini time arrived. Usher shut down the laptop and headed for the door. He stopped for a moment before heading back to the desk to install a high rated password in his computer. With Kalib Khan lurking around, he didn't want to take any chances.

As Usher sipped his martini, he wished Anasette were there. The bar was inhabited by a spectacularly uninteresting crowd. Forgoing a second, he passed on into the dining room to an equally mundane bunch of diners.

After an indifferent meal, Usher decided that a major part of the problem was of his own making. The fate of Alecia Arnold had cast a gloom over him. Maybe a movie would take his mind off the situation. On the way back to the room he bought a local newspaper for the TV Guide.

Picking the least objectionable of the movies offered, Usher sat back in his armchair, wishing he had had the foresight to pick up a bottle of brandy.

Usher revolved between watching the movie and dozing. Whichever state he was in was abruptly interrupted by what sounded like rapid hand slaps on the glass of the sliders and a low panicky call, "Orlop, Orlop, let me in. Orlop, Orlop, please let me in."

Instantly, Usher was out of his chair. A quick glance around the room didn't provide any immediate weapon, so he gripped his stainless steel-bodied ballpoint against his right palm and between the middle and ring fingers, which provided him with some protection.

The slapping and pleading persisted. The voice was familiar. If it hadn't been so stressed, he'd probably been able to identify the supplicant. Usher flipped off the lights before pulling back the drapery covering the sliders. There were only dim walkway lights illuminating the garden behind his ground floor room.

As soon as the drapery parted, a face pressed against the glass. Light from the TV offered sufficient illumination to recognize Kalib Khan.

Khan quickly glanced over his shoulder before saying, "Let me in. They are trying to kill me. Please, let me in. Please."

Usher opened the drapery a little more. He really didn't trust Kahn any further than he could dropkick him.

Kahn quit slapping the glass but continued mouthing his pleas.

If it was an act, it was a good one, complete with peed pants. Usher snapped the lock and pulled the door open far enough to let Kahn slide in. Kahn immediately closed and locked the door. Frantically, he covered the glass.

"Kahn, you're dripping on the carpet and, man, you stink. Get into the bathroom."

"Two men were going to kill me. He had his gun barrel at the base of my skull. Somebody scared them away. They may still be out there."

"Did they see you coming here?"

"I don't think so. They ran around the building before I got up."

"Okay, first get cleaned up." Usher handed him a wastepaper basket. "Empty your pockets into this. And get into the shower.... clothes and all and don't come out until everything is squeaky clean."

Kahn was shaking so badly he could hardly find his pockets.

"You want me to call the police?"

"No, who would believe me? I'm not very popular with the police."

Kahn was wearing a navy blue light jacket, black T-shirt, and jeans, black socks and tennis shoes. The jacket was the only garment left unsoiled. Kahn stashed the wastebasket, with his jacket stuffed on top, behind the toilet before getting into the tub shower. After he closed the glass door and turned on the water, Usher held his breath and retrieved the basket and flipped on the vent fan.

Usher turn the lights on again so he could investigate the contents of Kahn's pockets.

Usher turned the TV to a normal level in case the thugs were snooping around outside. That prevented a conversation with Kahn unless he moved closer, and that wasn't desirable at the moment.

Eventually, the shower went off. "Clean the bathroom floor before you come out," said Usher. Kahn wrapped himself in a fresh towel and used his sodden one to wipe the tile floor.

Kahn had regained much of his control before he came to stand in the bathroom doorway. He was no longer involuntarily flinching. He still presented a rather pathetic sight. He was about the same height as Usher but he was close to being called emaciated. He was carrying two other prominent keloidal scars. One was across the top of his left forearm and the other ran diagonally down his left peck.

To start off the conversation, Usher said "Sit down," indicating the desk chair, "and tell me why you are outside my room, after dark, with a bugging device in your pocket." Kahn looked at the display that Usher had made of his pocket items across the desk. Three sets of false ID from his billfold were stacked in neat little piles. The receiver and transmitter of a bug were side-by-side.

"What do you think?"

"Okay, tell me what happened out there."

"I counted rooms and found yours. I heard someone coming, so I stepped back in the bushes. Two guys came walking by and when they came even with me, both jumped at me. One said that if I even made a peep he put a hole through me. He was waving a gun in front of my face. Both of them grabbed me. The talking one said, "On your knees." As soon as I was on the ground one of them said, "Nothing personal, Kahn, but we got a job to do," as he jabbed a gun barrel to the back of my skull and cocked the thing.

"At that moment, a man and woman and a little kid came out of the unit just across the way. The one with the gun whispered 'Go'. They knocked me over one the ground. Both ran. I was hidden by the low hedge. No one saw me. When the coast was clear I started banging on your door."

"They knew who you were."

"Yeah, they knew my name."

"Then they must have followed you here."

Kahn hesitated for a moment.

"Come on. I know you're at the Holiday Inn. Who have you made mad enough to kill you?"

"I haven't fuzzed anyone up recently."

"You must be threatening someone on the Alecia Arnold affair."

"I haven't filed anything yet. There's no one that I'm threatening outside of maybe the murderer." Kahn stopped to think before going on. "Do you suppose the murderer might think that I can expose him?"

"I haven't the foggiest idea. Are you conducting an investigation on your own?"

"No, not really. I always keep a watch on anything that doesn't add up. The only thing I did was pick up a copy of the police report."

"You have a copy of the police report?"

"Yeah."

"Where?"

"In my room."

Usher retrieved his motel key card from the nightstand before stepping to the desk where he picked up Kahn's motel key card and his own laptop.

"What are you doing?" demanded Kahn.

"I want to read the crime report. You have one so I'm going to go get it. Where is it?"

"You can't do that. Those guys might be watching my place."

"I'll find out but I won't bring them back. Where's the report?"

"In my computer bag. You're going to leave me here alone?"

"If they have guns, I won't be any protection. Just don't wander around. I'll be back shortly. Then we'll figure out how to get you out of here."

As Usher picked up Kahn's keys, he said, "I wouldn't drive that rental car if I were you. It might be bugged, and as soon as you move, they'd have you. Next time I doubt if they'll give you any warning."

Under less trying circumstances, Kahn would have been screaming his head off if Usher had tried to pull this stunt, but he was still too shaken by his near-death experience.

Usher casually made his way to his rental car. He locked his laptop in the trunk. Even though it was password-protected he didn't want Kahn messing around with it.

No one followed Usher to the Holiday Inn. He passed the motel and turned into a Denny's parking lot next door. He walked around the building and across the adjacent parking lot, entering the hotel complex from the side. Numbers painted on the walls pointed him in the direction of Kahn's room, which was on the ground floor too.

A casual visual inspection of the central courtyard produced nothing that raised any suspicion. Usher sauntered to Kahn's room, put the card in the slot and stepped into the room. Light from the walkway was sufficient to briefly scan the place. The computer case was on the desk. Kahn was a messy guest. Clothes, food packages and newspapers were scattered all over the unit.

Usher closed the door and made sure it was locked. By the little light that penetrated the draperies, he picked up the case and quickly let himself out of the sliding door to the parking lot he'd just traversed. Two cars were being un-loaded down the way. As Usher was crossing the drive-through service lane to go around the restaurant, he heard the sound of running feet. A young man was racing through the breezeway. He stopped to first look left toward Kahn's room. His gaze passed on to the cars where luggage was being shifted. Nothing interested him in that direction. While looking back to the right he spotted Usher watching him.

Usher didn't wait for the guy to react. He turned back to the building, entered the dining room and walked out the far side. He'd parked in the space next to the exit, making it unnecessary to back up. The sculptor powered the car over the short stop, across the sidewalk and down the street into the darkness.

He was past mid-block before a figure charged out into the street. Usher drove with no headlights and when he went around the corner, he didn't brake so as to avoid giving away the taillight pattern.

After he was sure he was not being tailed, Usher pulled into a lighted parking lot to inspect the computer case. There was a little padlock on the zipper. Since he'd flown to California he didn't have his pocketknife or box cutter that he normally carried. Of course, he could always get into it one way or the other, but it might be more fun having Kahn hand him the report.

When he returned to his room, he put the card into the slot but the deadbolt had been thrown. "Okay, Kahn, open up and don't do anything stupid."

The bolt slid back and the door cracked open. Usher shoved it open with a toe. Khan had retreated to the bathroom door. Usher locked them in and put the computer case on the desk. "While you're getting me the police report, I'll tell you what I encountered while getting it." Kahn picked up his key ring from the desk to open the bag. From a folder he pulled out a four-page typed report.

"The maps, photos, the whole thing."

Khan took a much larger sheaf of papers out and handed them to Usher. "What happened?"

"You will won't be able go back to that motel and I'd abandon the car too." Usher went on to tell about his experiences.

"If you're telling the truth...."

"Listen warthog, watch who you are calling a liar."

"Sorry," mumbled Kahn. "If they knew you went in and then immediately left the back way, they must have my room bugged."

"I'd say that's a pretty good bet. Maybe your car too. It seems as if you've attracted a lot of interest. Are you trying to write an exposé on the murder? There are other strange things. I couldn't get a police report because there was supposed to be a computer glitch."

"That was no glitch," said Khan. "That was a massive computer failure that wiped everything including recent backups. There is a full-scale investigation into how and why."

"Did it have anything to do with the Arnold affair?"

Kahn shrugged. "As far as I know it was a coincidence, but it's strange that MVR has no record of Arnold's vehicle registration. No insurance information is available. Too many coincidences for my taste. Then there's the case of you and my cousin hobnobbing. You won't tell Sasha about this, will you?" The thought of Usher passing that info on to his family upset him. His look implored Usher to give assurances that his indignities wouldn't be told.

Not willing to throw away what might be a useful tool, Usher said, "It all depends on how I'm feeling towards you. Sasha and I met here and only because she thought I was a confederate of yours.

"I'll read this over a martini later." Usher went to his closet where he picked up a complementary plastic clothes bag, which he tossed to Kahn. "Put you wet clothes in this. I'll give you a shirt and pair of pants. I'll take you to a car rental agency. You have enough ID and credit cards so you shouldn't have any problem. From there you're on your own.

"While you're getting dressed tell me about your attackers."

"It was too dark to get a good look at them. They were young."

"How young?"

"Around 20. Maybe 22. They had baseball caps on but they had the current longish hair styles. Both had dark hair. Strong. Dark clothes. The one who spoke sounded like a beaner or a wop. The only thing I really had to look at was their shoes. They wore black sneakers, leather or vinyl. This only took a few seconds. I have the feeling that those guys were not pros, but I believe they could be lethal."

"It sounds like it," said Usher. "Grab your stuff and walk on my right side. You'll be in my shadow. Do you know where another car rental place is located?"

"Go down to the main drag to where the Holiday Inn is located and turn right. There are several down that way."

When Kahn finally spotted a satisfactory rental agency, Usher pulled up in front.

"What about my police report?" asked Kahn.

"You've already read it. If you can't remember it, I'll make a copy and give it back."

As Kahn stepped out of the car he said, "Thanks." It came out as if it was an attempt to say something in a foreign language. It certainly wasn't a common word in his lexicon. Usher was anxious to get to the police report. Also he wanted some quiet time to think about the attempt to kill Kahn. He stopped by a liquor store for a fifth of Beefeaters. He forsook the vermouth.

Armed with a bathroom glass of gin and the sheaf of papers that Kahn had handed over, Usher settled down in the easy chair with the TV turned off. He scanned through the papers. There was more than just the police report. He wondered if it was an oversight on Kahn's part or whether the reporter was trying to curry a bit of goodwill.

The first contact report rambled about quite a bit. Usher visualized a young, inexperienced officer trying to handle that type of crime scene. The shift commander's report was much more complete, although there were precious few facts.

About all that could be gleaned was that a man and his wife were taking a walk on the beach when they found the badly beaten body of Alecia Arnold lying on her back in the sand 23 feet from a small staircase leading to a public parking lot.

The victim had been dragged by her heels 212 feet through loose, dry sand. However, by the time the forensic officer had arrived, the crime scene was in a shambles. The discovering couple had walked over a considerable part of the dragline. Then they had milled around the body while waiting for the policeman, who did his bit, and then the place was further churned up by the medical personnel.

There were no usable footprints. There was no recognizable weapon or any other physical object that could be attributed to the assailant. No witnesses had been found.

An old Chevy sedan was in the parking area. Fingerprints showed that Arnold had driven it. Nothing of interest had been found there either. There was a slip showing that the car was registered to Ruth Lung. Later reports indicated that Ruth Lung had not been identified. Alecia's mother's name was Ruth Arnold, but no mother had stepped forward.

After Usher finished reading the police report, he had a feeling he'd just spent time eating a meal with no substance. He hadn't been satisfied. The only item that had caused Usher to raise an eyebrow was that Alecia had a single stainless steel ball bearing in her left rear pocket. That was the only thing in that pocket.

A diagram and photographs of the scene answered some of the questions Szedlak had raised. There was no hiding place for the body near where the assault had taken place. It would appear that there was an attempt to remove the body from the scene. The drag marks led to the parking lot.

The medical report indicated that there was only one weapon used in the attack. The marks left were peculiar in that there were deep bruises left by an instrument made of two ball-like objects about the size of ping-pong balls.

There were at least 20 blows to the body concentrated on or about the head and shoulders. There were also some strike bruises on the right arm and right leg. Indications were that the victim had tried to protect her head with her arms and then went down on her left side and curled into a fetal position. The skin was broken only when the bone was close to the surface.

Usher sipped his gin for a bit before going over a DNA lab report. The final report had been filed just two days earlier. It confirmed that it was a natural pregnancy in that the mother and the baby matched. They had the DNA of the father and it was being compared with male databases.

CHAPTER 6

Usher was awake but he was still in bed when Sasha called.

"I'm sorry to call so early. Bristol had to be here early to make the rounds. I wanted to catch you to see if that lunch offer was still on?"

"You bet. This is your territory. Why don't you pick a nice spot. We'll take my car, but you'll have to navigate."

"That sounds good to me. When?"

"Is 12 o'clock all right?"

"Great. I'll stop by your room at noon."

Usher used the morning to do some calling. He reported to Jangala on the current state of affairs. "I told you about the medical illustrator who is my old enemy's cousin. That old enemy is Kalib Kahn, the nasty reporter for 'The Orbiter'."

"The Orbiter?"

"Yes, that sensationalized tabloid you buy in the supermarket."

"I've heard of it in passing, but I'm not familiar with it."

"You're not missing anything. Kahn turns any story into something vulgar or evil. We had a couple of run-ins a while back.

"Last night there was a frantic slapping on my motel slider. Kahn was begging to be let in. Normally, I wouldn't have trusted him in my room but something had scared him sufficiently that he voided both sides. It seemed he was on his way to my room to install a bug."

"Why?"

"He's curious about why I'm here and he still isn't convinced that I'm not scheming against him with his cousin. He has a real paranoid streak."

"What scared him so badly?"

Usher related the story Kahn had provided. "In exchange for cleanup privileges, a shirt and pair of pants, plus safe passage to a car rental agency, I got Kahn's copy of the police report. Incidentally the police computer glitch turned out to be a massive systems failure.

"There was virtually nothing in the crime report of help. Apparently, Alecia Arnold was a 17-year-old, living on her own and she was starting to attend college. Her car was registered to a Ruth Lung. Does that name mean anything?"

"Alecia's mother was a 'Ruth'. But, Lung means nothing to me. She may have remarried. I'll do some checking. Ruth Arnold should still be alive. No obituary has ever surfaced. With all the publicity this case has had, she should have heard about it.

"Another little coincidence. A second computer failed so that California MVR has no registration information on Alecia's car. No insurance information has surfaced.

"This afternoon I'm going to wander down to Carmel and take a look at the crime scene. I'm beginning to feel somebody is panicking. It has to be pretty serious to want to eliminate a media figure."

"What about the baby?"

"I'm having lunch with Sasha Khan. I'm expecting to get a pretty complete report before I finish my salad."

Following Usher's conversation with Jangala, he called

Anasette. He knew she would find exquisite pleasure in Kahn's embarrassment. She'd grown a well earned dislike for the creep.

Sasha was punctual. Usher didn't know if she was remembering his chastisement or whether her arrival right on time meant she didn't need to say that she was sorry.

She gave Usher directions to a funky little restaurant that artistic types found convivial.

While in route, Sasha opened the conversation with a report on the condition of the infant. "They are calling her Baby A, which I don't like. It reminds me of the Scarlet A in a movie. Anyway, the poor little thing has been poked, prodded and stuck in every fashion imaginable and that whole lottery of specialists can't find anything wrong with her. If she had a mama, she could go home today."

Usher shook his head. "What a shame. Hell of way to start one's life. What happens now?"

"Bristol is temporarily in control. He'll keep her in the hospital until somebody shows up to claim her or the authorities take some action."

"Can't they find any family? Alecia was only 17."

"They can't find the mother, Rose Arnold. I understand Alecia's birth certificate has no father listed. No grandparents have been identified. Her school records haven't produced usable information either."

"There has to be a digital trail somewhere."

"You'd think so, but I haven't heard of any yet."

Lunch conversation turned into a lively art discussion. As they were preparing to leave Usher said, "How far is it to Carmel?"

"Not far....around 90 miles."

I'm going to take a little jaunt down there to look at the crime scene."

"For your friend?"

"That is a private itch I'm scratching. Unanswered questions bother me. I like to imagine various scenarios but I can't do that unless I have some facts to work with. I thought that I'd just plug in a few things that weren't in the police report."

"Are you trying to find a murderer?"

"No. I'll leave that to the authorities. When you're a sculptor you have a lot of brainless work that you have to do. I like to have something to think about during those times. Have you time to run down south?"

"Yeah. Bristol and I are going out for a late dinner after he finishes a meeting. Yes, I'd like to go."

"Do you need to pick up anything or can we leave from here?"

"Are you planning on coming back before I'd need a jacket?"

"That's the plan."

"Let's go."

CHAPTER 7

It was a pleasant drive through a new area for Usher. Sasha pointed out things of interest. She even knew about where they were going to find the beach access where the attack had taken place.

"How come you know the location?" said Usher.

"Bristol comes down here occasionally to play golf at Pebble Beach. I'm no golfer. I'd rather spend the time on the beach. I've been here several times. I have a pretty good collection of marine life drawings."

For part of Usher scenic tour, Sasha had him drive down the main street of Carmel with all of its quaint shops before they turned north along the beach

"That's Pebble Beach golf course in that direction. Are you a golfer?"

"No, never got around to it. From the looks of this area, you'd have to have a bit of money to play here."

Sasha smiled and nodded as she gave him a course correction. "The parking lot is just around the next bend."

The parking area was a long, narrow strip of land between the road and a little sea cliff. There were two lines of angled parking spots set nose to nose.

"For a weekday, the beach is well populated," said Usher, as he saw only a few vacancies out of the 40 or so places.

"Probably a lot of them are here because it is a murder scene."

"I wonder how much traffic there is at midnight."

"Never been here at night. On a weekday, in the winter.... probably not much."

Usher pulled into one of the empty slots. "Alecia's car was parked by the only lamppost....where the blue car is parked."

"She had to be meeting someone."

"Probably the father of her child."

"How do you figure that?"

"The sheriff couldn't find much money and having a baby costs some bucks. It must have been pretty important for her to drive this far at night and meet someone in a secluded place."

"But why this late in a pregnancy?"

"Maybe she was going to try to go it alone," said Usher. "There could be any number of reasons. We'll probably never know her real motives. It appears that she was pretty much a loner."

Usher and Sasha walked to the stairs leading to the beach. They were standing about 8 feet above the sand. Usher pointed out the direction of the drag marks.

"I don't think this was a planned murder," said Usher.

"Again, how do you figure that?"

"If I were planning a murder, it certainly wouldn't be here."

Sasha raised her eyebrow.

"These two staircases are the only access the beach for a long ways in both directions. The bank is too high with a steep incline. A hundred yards north the houses start and again in almost the same distance to the south. If your car was parked here and someone pulled into the lot, you wouldn't be able to get to it without being seen.

"The drag marks were coming to the north stairs."

"Maybe the person doing the dragging was trying to get her to a hospital," offered Sasha, a little hopefully.

"Maybe, but I rather doubt it."

Sasha raised another eyebrow.

"If you want to help....and for the sake of convenience, I'll call the assailant 'he,'....especially since I think the killer was probably the father of her child."

Sasha still looked dubious.

"Back to the original thought. Most everyone carries a cell phone....especially in an area like this. Do you have one?" asked Usher as he unsnapped his from his belt. Sasha fished around in her purse. "It would be quicker, easier and more attentive to Alecia's needs to call for help."

Usher continued. "He'd risk further injury by dragging her through the sand, especially by the heels with head flopping around."

"Wouldn't it be easier to drag her the other way around or carry her?"

"As for carrying, it's hard enough to walk in the loose, dry sand. Carrying that much additional weight would have become even more difficult. Maybe he wasn't strong enough to carry her."

"Aw, she was just a slip of a girl," said Sasha. "On the other hand, maybe he didn't want to get his clothes bloody."

"Yeah, that could've been the reason."

"Why do you think it was the father?"

"Because, he was running a big risk of discovery by trying to get the body off the beach. It would have been easier just to leave it. But he couldn't."

"The baby's DNA!"

"Right. And I bet the murderer lives somewhere around here."

Sasha turned to survey the homes of the area.

"Probably not immediately around here, but in the county. There is no mention that Alecia had any familiarities south of San Francisco. Any history that is known is from north of Frisco."

"Are you going down to the beach?"

Usher shook his head. "Everything can be seen better from up here. I have what I needed. Find us a good spot and I'll buy you a cold beer."

Sasha continued her tour guide service by pointing Usher in the direction of Pacific Grove, Cannery Row, ending up at Fisherman's Wharf in Monterey for that beer.

"Are you going to tell the authorities about your theories concerning the father?" said Sasha after the waiter was out of earshot.

"No, they undoubtedly have the same theory. It's the logical one from the information that's available. They're probably working on a DNA sample right now. Of course, there is the possibility that the father has never given a DNA sample."

"How would you like to live your life," said Sasha, "with the knowledge you will be connected with this case, even if you weren't the murderer, as soon as your DNA is put into the right databank?"

"No, thanks."

"What are you going to do now?" said Sasha.

"Tomorrow, I'll head north. I want to take a look at where Alecia lived. After that I'll probably return to Denver."

"I'll probably go home tomorrow too. Bristol is running out of excuses to keep me here. My stay could probably have been longer if there had been something wrong with Baby A. As it stands now this isn't much of a job."

"How so?"

"It's a simple and very common C-section not worthy of paying for my services. Bristol does want some work done on what the pathologists just found. There were three blows from whatever weapon was used that could have caused the mother's brain damage."

"Sorry to hear your job fizzled."

"Oh, I have enough work that I've been putting off to keep me pretty busy."

****

In the morning, Usher was ready to check out and hit the road to Petaluma as soon as the rush-hour slacked off. He googled Alecia's address for a map. He printed a copy on his cheap little printer. There was the letter "B" after the house number, indicating a multiple dwelling.

As it turned out, the address belonged to a large older frame structure....a utilitarian looking place. There was a basement halfway underground with two stories on top. Instead of a porch, steps led up to a raised entry with a glassed in office on the right. On the left wall were four metal mailboxes. In response to Usher's doorbell summons a matronly woman with flour on her forearms greeted him.

"Yes?"

"My name is Usher Orlop. I am a guardian ad litem to Baby A, the daughter of Alecia Arnold. We have a beautiful little baby girl down in San Jose without a mother and I am trying to find any relative."

"I read about that in the paper. Poor thing. Alecia was a nice little girl....so pretty. I really don't know much about her. She was with us for about six months."

"You know how she lived?"

"She had to wait each month for a small check from somewhere. When the check came in, she paid her rent in cash. There wasn't much left over. She took any little job that would pay. Until she was obviously pregnant, she worked at one of the coffee houses where they make those frothy drinks."

"Did Alecia ever mention any family? Or the father of her baby?"

"No, she never mentioned any family, and she was pregnant when she got here. I didn't really know, but I always figured she came from over on the coast."

"Alecia rented a room or apartment from you?"

The lady smiled rather proudly. "We have three one-room apartments here. And when my husband, retires we'll make the garage over into two more. This is our retirement plan."

"It looks as if you have a nice, neat operation here. Congratulations."

"Oh my, I have to finish punching down that dough. If you need any more information, you will have to follow me to the kitchen."

As Usher trailed along behind, he took note of the tidy, sanitized interior. There was not much evidence of the personalities of the occupants. He had to mentally smile at the old-fashioned kitchen. It was nothing like his ultramodern gourmet facility, but she could do everything that he could do. The difference was that he pressed a button and she had to turn a crank.

The bread maker rolled a wad of dough out onto a floured table, cut it into quarters and proceeded to vigorously punch it down.

"Our three apartments are in the half-basement. One is under the front porch. The other two are behind it. They all share a bathroom. They're not very big, but it's much cheaper than regular apartments."

"Have you cleaned Alecia's apartment yet?"

"No. Her rent isn't up for a couple of days. The Petaluma police brought a Monterey sheriff's deputy here to take a look at it. They took her computer and anything they felt might be of use. They even took the stuff out of her garbage can and wastepaper basket. You won't find much."

"They were looking for a murderer and I'm looking for a family. I also would like to find out how she lived....what was important to her."

"If it'll help that poor little baby. Take the key hanging under D on the board by the door over there. That's the basement door. One occupant, Milli, will be home. She's a little strange but harmless. Don't step on Sir Laurence, Milli's cat."

When Usher stepped into the stairway he paused for a moment to let his eyes adjust from the bright light in the airy kitchen to the dim basement. When he reached the bottom step, he stopped to get his bearing. There was an exterior door to the stairwell to his right. Ahead was a partially open door to unit C. To the left was a closed door with a bathroom sign on it. Further to the left at the end wall was D.

Just as Usher was about to head for Alecia's unit, he felt a movement against his right leg. A cat that was under the staircase was sniffing his leg. Usher extended the back of his right hand for the smeller.

Usher had always gotten along with cats. Leaving his feet planted where they were and his hand still in position, Usher slowly seated himself on the step.

"Why, hello, big boy. Aren't you a grand one? You must be Sir

Lawrence."

A very large, long haired cat crawled out next to Usher's foot. Except for a little white snip on his chest, the feline was coal black. When Usher turned his hand over to scratch under the jaw, he was rewarded with a loud purr.

"Sir Lawrence, are you bothering the man?"

Peering around the edge of the C apartment door was the head of a woman of indeterminate age other than to say maybe middle aged. She wore out-of-fashion large lens glasses. Her hair had not been brushed after she had gotten out of bed

"That's all right. We're just getting acquainted."

The head disappeared. Usher could hear some scrambling around in the apartment. Shortly, the woman stepped out into the hall. She had run a brush through her hair and put on a long robe.

Usher stood up. "Hi. I'm Usher Orlop. I'm a guardian ad litem trying to find Alecia Arnold's family. I suppose you know all about the case."

"Yes. The area TV stations have covered the case on a day-by-day basis. Terrible."

"We have a beautiful little baby girl needing a home. Do you know anything about Alecia's family situation or anything about the father? Ms...."

"I'm Milli. The police asked me the same questions, but I wouldn't tell them anything because when I came out of my room, the deputy sheriff was pointing his finger at Sir Lawrence and cocked his thumb and shot him. He bragged to the other policeman that he shot cats when he was on night patrol. Every time they asked the question, I told them I didn't know." Milli patted her chest and Sir Lawrence leapt into her arms. "I'm not going to help anyone who wants to shoot my Sir Lawrence."

"Maybe dealing with criminals all the time warps their outlook on life. Me, I'm a pushover for cats. Do you know anything about Alecia that might help find a home for Alecia's baby?"

"Alecia never talked about herself. She was a nice person having a bad time."

"Do you have any idea the source of Alecia's money?"

"She couldn't work enough to pay her way, being pregnant and going to school full-time. I know she had some assistance for tuition and books. Each month she received a check in the mail. I think it was from her mother, but I'm not sure. Then something happened this month. Each month she would anxiously await the check. When the letter came she'd be greatly relieved. This month, when the envelope arrived, she went into deep despair. I'm guessing that there was no check.

"For several nights she cried herself to sleep. I could hear her when I went to the bathroom."

"You know from where the letters were sent?"

"You can't see the letters unless you open the box and it's against the law to mess with someone else's mail."

Usher raised an eyebrow and scratched Sir Lawrence under the chin.

"I did see an Indonesian stamp once."

"Do you have any idea why Alecia went to Carmel?"

"No. I heard her leave late in the afternoon. I didn't think anything about it until I heard about her on the morning news."

"Do you think the tenant who lives in the front could know something that might help?"

"He is a merchant seaman. He's gone for three or four months at a time. He's been gone for weeks."

"Is there anything else you know that might help me?"

Millie mulled the question around for a time.

Usher could tell she did, but she was debating whether or not to divulge it. Usher scratched Sir Lawrence again, which produced a loud purr.

"The police took most everything," said Millie, "but I don't think they got it all."

"How so?"

"Both Alecia's apartment and mine have a little half wall between the range and the sitting area. It keeps the grease from splattering on the big chair. There is a board on top that can be lifted off. I told Alecia about it. We keep our valuable stuff in there."

Millie went on. "I didn't tell the police. I wasn't going to help that cat killer." She lifted Sir Lawrence up so she could bury her face in his fur.

Usher figured that was about all the information Milli could provide unless he came up with some specific questions. "Thanks, Milli. I hope we'll find someone to give that little girl a loving home."

Milli scampered back into her room with Sir Lawrence and closed the door.

Usher unlocked Alecia's room and swung the door open. It went all the way to the wall. He stepped into the room far enough so we could see the whole thing. He shook his head. The second closet at home was about the same size as this apartment. On his right side was a two-place table with a pair of straight-backed chairs. Behind the table was a small refrigerator. Moving counterclockwise around the room there was a small counter space, corner sink, counter space, apartment size range, Millie's wall, easy chair, small side table, chest of drawers and a wardrobe closet along the end wall. Continuing on the entry door side of the room there was a bedside table, a single bed sticking out into the room and the space behind the door.

Alecia didn't appear to be overly concerned with housekeeping. Of course, a police search may have contributed to the appearance. Usher suspected homework was done on the dining table. There was a glass containing pens and pencils and a cord hanging down from a small printer on a shelf above. However, there was no computer. The wastepaper basket was empty.

Usher gave the room a slow search. Nothing of obvious value presented itself. He hadn't really expected anything but he did pick up some impressions of the former occupant. No affluence was visible. Her clothes and shoes were from Goodwill or discount houses, except for an expensive well-worn pair of hiking boots. There was no TV. The radio was tuned to the public radio station. There was a walking stick in the corner and a small backpack in the closet. The hiding spot was left until last.

The wall was made of concrete blocks with a plaster coating on the living room side. The wall was about 5 feet high and extended two blocks away from the outer wall. A stained 1 x 10 fir board covered the top. Using a couple paper towels to cover this part of the operation, Usher removed the radio and a couple of large pinecones from the surface. The top fit well with no play. It resisted removal until Usher pulled it away from the wall a half an inch. Under the lid were four holes in the blocks. Usher was tall enough to be able to see into the spaces. There were floors in each. The hiding place had been made intentionally.

Sidling around behind the easy chair, Usher could see down into all the holes. The first contained a coffee house cup with some currency and change. Using a pencil to move the bills around he counted $23. Beside the cup was an airmail envelope standing on its end. It was quite thick and it had an Indonesian stamp and return address. He picked it out of the brick. Since he planned on taking with him he did not worry about fingerprints. It was from Ruth Lung. Inside were torn up bits and pieces of the letter.

The second hole was stuffed full of pay stubs and bills.

The third had a tear sheet from the San Francisco Chronicle. The story was two weeks old. It reported that Judge Manuel Sautto of the Second Federal District Court in California had been selected by the new president to fill the vacancy on the Supreme Court. There was a photo of the judge in his robes inset into a larger photograph of the judge and his family. The group shot had been taken at a poolside function with many people in the background. The judge and his wife were arm in arm. The judge had his other arm around his daughter Lisa, who looked to be about 15. The mother, Carmen, had her arm around the waist of her son Rufino. Both of the kids were wearing bathing suits.

The item of interest was that the son had a hole poked in his stomach. Usher guessed a ballpoint pen had been used because of the fine ink line on part of the tattered paper. He set the article aside with the letter.

Under the papers was an open jewelry box. It had not been for a ring since there was no slot. Whatever it had contained had left dimples in both the top and the bottom. Usher left the box untouched.

The final hole was a catchall for little bits of Alecia's life. Usher stirred around with the pencil, but nothing on which he could place any value appeared.

After replacing the lid and rearranging the items on top, Usher pulled a sheet of paper from the printer. He wrapped the envelope and newspapers sheet in the paper. The little packet went under his waistband in the back. He pulled his shirt down to hide his find.

Usher let himself out of the apartment locking the door behind him. Sir Lawrence was in the hallway. The tail went straight up and he came over to sideswipe Usher's leg. "Hi, big boy," said Usher as he stooped to scratch the cat's ears."Sir Lawrence, behave yourself. Don't bother the man" said Millie who was peering around the doorjamb.

"No bother. Thanks for the tip on the hidi-hole. There were some personal items in there but nothing of any particular value. The police didn't find it. I wouldn't say anything about it, so your hiding place will still be safe."

Milli clicked her tongue to call Sir Lawrence. She scooped him up in what Usher took to be a loving embrace.

"Aren't you concerned that Sir Lawrence might get out when someone opens the door?"

"No, his first owner declawed him so he's afraid to be outside. He's happy to be with me. I'll keep him safe."

"He's lucky to have you," said Usher as he went up the stairs to the kitchen. He knocked on the door to announce his arrival. The landlady was still in the kitchen.

"Come in. Did you find anything to help?"

"The police were pretty thorough. At least I got a sense of what kind of world Alecia lived in. Well, you'd better clean out the refrigerator and save yourself some stinky work. Alecia is not coming back and this isn't a crime scene. The police have already gotten everything of help out of it. I'd clean it up and get another tenant."

"You're right, but we were afraid do anything until somebody said to."

Usher took his leave. He was anxious to piece the letter together. He'd been uncertain what to do next. As soon as he found out what was in the letter and investigated the article, he'd make a decision on his next move.

To put that letter together again, he'd need a lot of cellophane tape. He headed back toward the business district. He stopped at the first convenience store for a couple rolls of tape. Since the store was featuring a gourmet coffee bar, Usher exited with a large cup.

He needed somewhere to work on the letter. A windy picnic table wasn't it. He went to motel row and checked into a midrange accommodation. If he needed to stick around, he'd have a place to stay. If there was nothing left to do in the area, he'd go back to San Jose and then catch a flight out for Portland or Denver, whichever seemed appropriate.

Sticking the tape in his pocket, he picked up his coffee before heading to the hotel desk. After registration he went directly to his room. He'd juggle the car around after he made his plans.

In his room, he turned on the classic cable station and retrieved the packet. After dumping the envelope of pieces on the desk, he inspected the contents more thoroughly. Alecia had torn the whole thing up into half-inch squares. The paper had been a lightly tinted blue tear-off sheet from a pad. There was writing on both sides. The handwriting was in English and in a fairly legible script. It was going to be like putting a jigsaw puzzle together without any large, interlocking pieces.

Just as Usher started sorting out the edge pieces, the telephone rang. Since no one knew he was there, it must be the desk.

"Yes?

"Orlop. Those two guys that jumped me are headed up the stairs to your unit. Go!"

"Usher didn't bother to wonder how Kahn knew where he was. He swept the letter pieces into the envelope. Stuffed everything into a pocket and let himself out on the balcony. This time he was on the second floor. He slung over the wrought-iron rail. Holding onto the verticals, he let himself slide down to the bottom. The drop to the patio below was only three or so feet. He hit the ground in full flight back toward his car.

Keying the lock before he reached the car permitted him to be in the car and moving within moments. He turned right with the traffic. Usher didn't know what kind of car his visitors had, but nothing followed him out of the motel lot. However, another car that he suspected was Kahn's pulled out of the next motel lot. After Kahn had changed cars in San Jose, Usher had no idea what he was driving.

As soon as traffic permitted, Kahn move closer so Usher could make an identification and then dropped in behind Usher's car.

Usher turned into a parking lot of a large barbecue restaurant and pulled behind the building. Kahn followed him around, parked, and came up to the passenger side of the car. Usher unlocked the door.

Kahn's first words were, "I think we're even now. You didn't tell Sasha?"

"Of course, I didn't see any bad guys, but I'll take your word for it as soon as you tell me how this thing all came about."

"I drove up here from San Jose to check on Arnold's digs and I spotted two guys apparently watching the house. They looked too close to what I saw of the guys at your motel. I held back to watch them. And who should turn up but a disinterested sculptor. When you left, they followed you and I followed them.

"At the motel, one followed you to see what room you had. When he found out, he went back to the car to pick up his buddy. When they headed in your direction, I called."

"Thanks. Who do you think they are? How sure are you that they are the ones who attacked you?"

"I have no idea who they are. From their looks and actions I'd say they're Hispanic, but I haven't done anything on the Mexican or Colombian cartels for a long time. I'm not involved in any of the drug trade. I haven't even been writing about it lately.

"It looks like you're on their list now, too. I know they took your license number. Did you register under your own name?"

"Yes. I can easily be found."

"Did you get anything of interest from that apartment?"

"Only impressions. The police had been there earlier and they took her computer, papers, contents of a wastepaper basket.... everything except some clothes and toiletries. Come to think of it, there were no supplements and she seemed to be a health nut, from the contents of the refrigerator. The police probably took those too. There was some hiking equipment too.

"I did find out she had been getting a small check each month, but it didn't come this month."

"Oh," said Kahn as he tried to raise his eyebrows. "Daddy

missed his monthly payment, huh? She went down to Carmel to bounce him on it and he killed her."

"That's entirely possible I guess, but where does this strong-arm pair come in? If some kid knocked her up and can only pay a small amount each month, where does the money come from to hire hit men and screw up police computers?"

"Good question. I thought you had a passing interest in this thing, but you're acting like a dick....yesterday Carmel, today Petaluma. Where to next?"

Usher thought for a moment. "I've scratched my curiosity about enough. I still wonder why Alecia had a ball bearing in her hip pocket. I would think it would be uncomfortable to sit on when she drove all that way. There are a few more little things but I will have to defer to the thug problem. I need to shake them off my tail. I'm going to head for San Francisco and turn in this car.

"Are you going back to the motel?"

"No, I never downloaded any gear."

Kahn looked his question.

"I had to use the bathroom," said Usher. "Give me a phone number in case anything comes up."

Kahn pulled out a business card and wrote a number on it. "My cell. I already have your numbers." Kahn smiled.

Usher checked his back trail to make sure no one would follow. Contrary to what he told Kahn, he needed to piece the letter together before leaving the area. He stopped at an ATM to get cash so he wouldn't need to use his credit card at another motel.

In Santa Rosa, Usher found an older hotel off the beaten path that had a lot of trees, hedges and privacy. Under an assumed name he took a ground floor room where he could see his parking spot.

With the curtains open so he could see if anyone took interest in his car, Usher began putting the letter together. He resisted reading any of the tight little scratch marks until it was in one piece.

It was martini time before he finished. Before starting to decipher the letter, Usher retrieved his bottle Beefeaters from the car. Over a gin, he tried to make sense out of the letter. After the third go-around, the story began to come together. Lung was not a body organ but the Chinese name of Alecia's mother's new husband. The couple had recently moved to Jakarta, Indonesia. The husband was a devout Muslim, and Ruth, her mother, had converted to Islam. Now she would have to change her ways. She could no longer withhold the money from the household account so that she could send Alecia's check. That would be the same as stealing from her husband. Also she had told her husband of Alecia's pregnancy because the mother had been committing the sin of omission.

Ruth told her daughter that she was fortunate that there was an ocean between her and her stepfather. He had gone into a towering rage, threatening a ritual killing to cleanse the family. The husband had forbidden any further connection between the mother and her evil child.

Usher settled back to ponder the mental state of Alecia, a 17-year-old, cast out by mother, broke, and about to have a baby. That was no way to meet adulthood.

At least it was evident she hadn't gone to Carmel to dun the father for a monthly check.

Usher picked up that torn out article. On closer examination the initial stab had been in the groin area and the pen had traveled further north before punching through the paper. The son, Rufino, was reported in the article to be 20 years old.

When Usher ran down the home address, the clipping took on new meaning.... Carmel, California. This revelation set up a whole new set of scenarios. Is the young Mr. Sautto the father of Alecia's child?

With her small source of income gone, maybe Alecia decided to put the squeeze on the one she'd stabbed in the genitals. If he's the one, why wait so long? Of course, now would be a good time because pop will be under close scrutiny during the confirmation hearings and an illegal pregnancy in the family wouldn't fly well.

This might be the source of the goons who had followed him. His first concern was to shake them. They'd be able to get his name and home address from either the motel or the car rental agency.

With that thought in mind, Usher pulled out his cell phone and punched in Anasette's number.

"Bout time I heard from you. You having so much fun that you forgot your old friends?"

"What are you talking about? I called you yesterday," said Usher in an indignant tone.

"Ya, yesterday morning and this is today afternoon. You could've gotten in a whole heap of trouble in that length of time."

"Well, yes, I do have had a bit of a problem. It looks as if those two thugs that jumped Kahn are now on my trail."

"You're kidding. You mean the ones that were going to blow his brains out?"

"Kahn thinks so. He's the one that spotted them and warned me."

"And you believed Kahn?"

"At the moment I couldn't afford not to believe him. They supposedly tailed me away from Alecia's apartment. If I'm of any interest to their boss, my name and address can be easily obtained. Keep an eye open for anything suspicious. If something doesn't look right, call Szedlak."

"When are you coming back?"

"I think I've done all I can around here. I can probably do more with Jangala's LexisNexis account than I can do here. However, I don't want to lead them to him. I'll go back to San Francisco, turn in the rental car and fly to wherever I can get to the fastest....Seattle, Boise, Salt Lake. And then catch another flight to Portland. I'll probably spend a day or two there and then come home."

"Hurry back. I want a steak at Fahrenheit 451."

CHAPTER 8

By the time Usher made it to Portland, he was beat. He had dozed in the airport while awaiting connections. He needed a shower and a shave badly. It had taken him 18 hours to get from San Francisco and Portland.

Before attacking the problems of eating, transportation and lodging, he called Jangala. He'd given Little Tyrant a much abbreviated summary of his trip to Alecia's apartment. He didn't want to present his own impression on the letter. He felt it would be better for Jangala to look at the raw material. Maybe he would come to a different conclusion.

"Usher. Are you in town?"

"Yes, I'm at the airport. I want to take a taxi to some other car rental agency rather than use an airport office. It would be harder to check on my movements."

"Stay there. I'll send a car for you. How long do you plan on staying?"

"A day or two. Will you give me access to your LexisNexis account? I have some things to look up."

"In that case, I'll have Annikki make up a room for you. Stay here and you can use my machine." Arrangements were made for a pickup in 45 minutes. Usher headed for baggage.

At the house, Mrs. Kalunki met Usher and took him directly to the office. Jangala was pushing himself in his big chair back from the computer to his desk. Without asking, Mrs. Kalunki served two cups of coffee.

"How's the baby?"

"The last word I had was that she was doing fine. I hear she's a hospital pet."

Never one to waste time, Jangala asked for a full report of Usher's California activities. Usher wearily set his cup back in the saucer.

Jangala's eyes followed every move. "However, first things first," said Jangala as he rang for the housekeeper. "Annikki, please show Usher to his room so he can clean up and rest until dinner is served."

To Usher he said, "You have about three hours. Would you like a snack now or would you rather wait until supper?"

A greatly relieved sculptor said, "Let me take my coffee with me and I'll be good until later."

Usher had a shower and then flopped onto the bed. He was immediately asleep. The dinner wake-up call came all too soon, but he made it downstairs in good time. Jangala was already at the table. Another setting was to his right.

"For my hearing, the other end of the table is too far away." Uncharacteristically, the host engaged in small talk.

Usher asked, "How are Tanner and Lyyli doing?"

"It appears I have given them a monumental chore. We moved the operation into a vacant commercial building the corporation owns. Tanner drives in every Friday morning and stays until Sunday afternoon. Then he takes work home to do during the week.

"I've set up facilities in the building so he can camp out over the weekend. Lyyli lives close enough. She'd rather drive home."

"Are they pleased with what they are finding?"

"They are ecstatic. It seems as if Henna was a fine recorder of people and places. Unfortunately, she didn't make any records of what she was shooting. They always have a great stack of prints they want identified. I can help them on some, and the others I don't recognize."

Jangala ordered coffee to be served in the office. Apparently, the old man was now comfortable enough around Usher to no longer hide his walking gyrations. When they settled down in the office, Jangala ordered Usher to report.

The full telling of the tale took a long time, with Jangala's periodic interruptions for clarification and sidebar thoughts.

When Usher reached the part where he searched the Alecia's apartment, he produced the taped-together letter and the newspaper article concerning Judge Sautto. These he lay on the desk for Jangala to read.

When Jangala finished absorbing the material, he said, "I found a record of Ruth's marriage to Lung, but I didn't realize he was Chinese. She must be mentally retarded to marry a Muslim and take his faith."

Usher voiced his suspicion that the Sautto kid could be the father of Alecia's baby. "If we can get a DNA sample from him, we could settle that question."

"Do you know where the kid is now?"

"No, all I have is this article. He doesn't seem to fit in with what little information we have on the thugs that jumped Kahn and supposedly tracked me. There is a possibility that they are Hispanic and the kid is of Mexican descent. That's the only vague connection that we have."

"There has to be another element. How do you suppose the twenty-something-year-old kid can throw around enough weight to make computer systems crash and hire hit men?"

"He has a powerful father."

"But to do something that destructive, the judge would have to know that his son is involved in serious activities that would keep him off of the Supreme Court.

"We really don't have enough information to make even an educated guess. Let me wander around online to see what I can find." To change the subject, Usher asked, "Are you planning to intervene on the baby's behalf?"

"I don't see how I can be of any benefit now. The state will take care of her until she can be adopted. Important thing is that she gets a loving home. I can keep an eye on her and intervene if necessary."

"If you'll pardon my pointing it out, you may not have enough time to sit back to see if she has fair-weather sailing. Would you be interested in setting up a permanent provision for her if I can provide a good loving home?"

"I would suspect that you are not talking about yourself. You have someone in mind?"

"Yes, but I'll hang onto the name until I'm sure that the couple is willing and able."

"Why not? I can't use all of my money. However, I want to know all about the situation before I commit."

"I'll have to have some time in Denver to check on it. I'll let you know."

After coffee, Usher declined using Jangala's iMac because he didn't want to be that close to the boss's personal data. He opted to use his wireless laptop. All he wanted was a password to access the Nexis. He also preferred to work at the desk in his room to avoid distractions. Despite her stern exterior demeanor, Annikki had a tendency to cluck over Jangala and, as Usher's relationship with the old man tightened, Usher was finding himself under the same wing.

From the article, he entered searches for the judge, his wife, son, and daughter and came up with tons of hits.

Usher started to read. He set up a file into which he copied items he wanted to print. After a couple of hours of scanning through articles on the judge, Usher felt he had a pretty good handle on that personality.

Skipping along, he picked up a vague portrait of the wife and the 17-year-old daughter. He didn't spend much time on them because his main interest was Rufino.

Surprisingly for one so young, Rufino had a substantial paper trail. There was nothing critically serious, but as Usher moved through the various articles and reports, a general flavor began to emerge. Rufino was on the fringe edge of trouble. Apparently, he wasn't sufficiently involved to get slapped with any of the consequences.

Another thought occurred to Usher. Because of his lineage he might be shielded. Sautto's name would appear in the initial sweep of a teenage booze party, but when penalties were meted out he was absent.

Usher poked around until he was able to pull up images of Rufino. He'd been a cute little kid with a thick bush of slightly wavy dark hair, large dark eyes set in a light olive skin. As time went along, he became a handsome youth who looked much younger than his chronological age.

Going back into the newspaper articles, Usher started making a timeline of activities. The most recent reported activities were in Hermosillo, Mexico. The first Mexican report was about 18 months earlier. It seemed that young Sautto commuted between Southern California and the Hermosillo area.

The results of the whole evening's inquiry were only some vague feelings. A fuzzy image of an apprentice loser and Playboy presented itself. The types of places and the persons with whom his name was associated pointed in that direction, as did the hours of the night when he seemed to be active.

Usher finally signed off. He went down to see if Jangala might still be up at that late hour. He was. The door to the den was open and the old man was sitting before the large iMac screen. Usher started to tap on the door to announce his presence when Jangala motioned toward the liquor cabinet and said, "Help yourself."

"Thanks." Usher opened the cabinet and was faced with an array of brands far beyond his budget. Off to the side he spotted a bottle of Old Overholt rye whiskey, which was more his speed. Usher picked up a lead crystal highball glass, figuring that it represented more money than his and Anasette's monthly booze bill.

Usher sloshed a healthy portion into the glass before asking, "Can I get you something?"

"Yes, some of the same as you. That's my private stash. I'm just showing off with the fancy stuff."

Usher took a seat in front of the big desk. Jangala swiveled his chair about to face him.

"How was your search?"

"No great revelations, but some tantalizing tidbits. The whole Sautto family gets more than its share of ink. The judge is always in some sort of controversy, usually connected to a far out liberal ruling from the bench. The wife makes her splash by being seen, not by what she does. The son, Rufino, appears on the cusp of being in trouble, but never charged."

"That doesn't surprise me," said Jangala. "If one knows how to play the game, most anything can be swept out of sight.... especially, when one has money and influence." There was a slight smile on his face. As the old man glanced toward Usher the smile disappeared. "But once in a while it doesn't work."

Usher knew that the old man was thinking about the loss of his only grandson and how Usher had started that chain of events.

"It would seem," said Usher, continuing this line of thought, "that young Sautto spends a lot of time in Mexico. It sounds as if he is too young with too much money and too much freedom."

"I'm familiar with that child-rearing formula. It has a low success potential. While you were working on that, I was doing my homework."

Usher smiled.

"I called the attorney who did the paperwork on Jon and Eric. This baby thing is rather delicate. As far as I can tell, there is no one in that line that can put me in it. I want to keep it that way. I especially don't want Alice Lung to know. She has a history of doing anything to improve he own security. The man she married is a moderately wealthy businessman and as long as she toes the line, her husband will care for her at a level befitting his social standing. That is probably why she severed her ties with her own daughter. I don't want that woman to ever get a sniff of the Jangala name.

"However, I cannot let that be the excuse for not doing what needs to be done. After all, Nyla is my great, great, great granddaughter."

"Nyla?"

"That little girl was never properly named and I've always liked Nyla, so I'll use it to designate Alecia's daughter."

"Nyla suits me fine. What are you having the attorney do?"

"He's just familiarizing himself with the situation and coming up with various actions that might be used to gain control over Nyla. We need an objective before we can initiate anything."

"As soon as I can book a flight to Denver, I'll be taking off."

"Make up a bill for me and I'll have Annikki make out a check for you."

"That may not be a good idea. We could be dealing with somebody with enough clout to get into my bank account and it wouldn't be a good idea to have your check in my account at this time."

"You're right. Give me your account number and I'll have an untraceable transfer made."

Chapter 9

Anasette met Usher at the airport. The petit former classical dancer was decked out in her multilayered winter garb, which made her look like an overweight teddy bear. Anasette was never one to engage in public displays of affection. A one-arm hug around the waist would have to suffice until later.

After picking up his luggage, the pair headed for the parking garage, where Anasette relinquished the keys to Usher's treasured classic Shelby Mustang. Usher had an ambivalent attitude towards the drive back into the city. It was a miserable long trip over snowy, salted roads. He didn't like to expose the undercarriage of his Mustang to the ravages of salt, but he relished any opportunity to drive his car beyond the city streets. The long drive also gave Anasette time to squeeze Usher for the complete story of his adventures. The relating helped Usher to organize his thoughts.

Anasette already knew most of the story. Usher filled in all of the blanks except for his thoughts concerning finding a home for Nyla. He wanted to think on that a bit longer.

Usher turned into the alley behind his studio. He fingered the garage door control. He had to slow to let the industrial-size truck door rise. As he turned to lineup with the entry into this building, Usher was aware of a movement further down the alley.

He eased the Mustang toward the interior parking area. There was a squall of tires. A car was turning in from the alley behind him. Usher stopped about halfway into the garage.

The car behind came to an abrupt stop and the passenger door flew open. "We've got company," warned Usher.

He hit the garage door button again to close the door. There wasn't enough room between the following car and the loading dock for the passenger's door to open fully. Usher could see a bulky male figure struggling to get out.

As the door descended, Usher jumped the Mustang forward into the building. He revved the engine, giving the shockingly loud characteristic cackle.

"Call 911," yelled Usher. Anasette was out of the car in a flash and darted into her apartment.

The other car lurched forward to block the descending door. Normally, when the garage door hit an object it would reverse itself and rise. However, when the door came in contact with the hood, the motion of the car brought the windshield against the door, snapping the wheels of the door out of their tracks.

Usher could see both car doors open. He rolled down his window so he could reach an electrical box on the left wall.

This was one of Usher's hiding spots. An electrical box was mounted on a pin so it could swing sideways exposing a niche, where he kept some artillery. Usher grabbed the .44 Ruger Blackhawk Magnum with his left hand and shifted it to his right, making it possible to shoot back over his left shoulder. His first shot went through the garage door and he heard glass go.

When a .44 Magnum goes off in a confined space it makes everyone in the vicinity aware of its power. His second shot went through the open driver's door. That convinced the two assailants not to hang around. They each put a retaliatory shot into the garage door as they ran.

With the overhead door jammed into the car, there were still openings into the building. Usher didn't want to chance an entry, so he kept an eye on the door as he moved over to Anasette's apartment.

He tapped on the door. "Anasette."

"The cavalry is on its way," came a voice through the door.

"I think they've gone, but I'm going to watch until the troops arrive."

Usher heard Anasette talking to the dispatcher. "The bad guys have gone. No more gunfire."

Sirens were off in the distance and approaching fast. Darkness had fallen, so Usher turned on the loading dock lights.

Anasette stayed in the warmth of her studio. By the time the police arrived, Usher was certainly ready for the cup of coffee that she passed out to him. He was getting cold.

Usher met the officer on the loading dock. He gave them the story of what happened. The officers inspected what proved to be a rental car. Usher's shot had gone through the windshield and the rear window.

While they were waiting for the crime scene team to look over the car, reports started coming in that there had been a carjacking a block away. Two young Hispanic males pulled an old woman out of her car and left her lying in the street.

One of the officers came over to Usher, who was watching activities. "Lieutenant Szedlak is coming over." Usher stuck his head into Anasette's studio. "Szedlak is on his way over. Will you go upstairs and start the coffee? Lock your door before you leave."

While the police were still present, Usher snapped a few photos for the insurance guy. Then he took the elevator down to the studio. He pulled out a couple of sheets of 4 x 8 plywood to secure the building. When he returned to the ground floor, he knew that Szedlak was on the scene due to the crisp execution of the investigational functions.

"You're going to need a new door," said Szedlak as he came around the corner from the loading dock. "What have you been up to now?"

Usher bobbed his head upward. "It probably ties in with the police report you couldn't get. Anasette is upstairs. She was with me when this unfolded this evening, but she doesn't know what happened."

Turning to the sergeant, Szedlak said "Get a tow truck over to get that thing out of here. Post a car outside until the owner can secure the building. I'll be upstairs talking to the passenger."

By the time the elevator disgorged the two men in Usher's pad, Anasette had three mugs of coffee poured. One sat on either side of her place at the dining bar.

"Hi, Lieutenant." To Usher she said, "What took you so long?"

"Just guarding the keep to protect the resident damsel."

"You said this related to the missing police report....Carmel?" said Szedlak.

"I think so." Usher gave the lieutenant a brief, censored report on his California adventures. Szedlak had encountered Kalib Kahn on one of his early run-ins with Usher and he took great glee in Kahn's embarrassment.

"So you think these goons are the same ones that Kahn claims assaulted him and followed you. You may be getting soft in the head. Kahn might have set up the whole thing."

"I don't think so. There is no benefit in it for him. A story just to embarrass me isn't worth the effort. Kahn isn't a good enough actor to pull off that assault story. I know he will do anything to get a good story....even make it up, but as far as I am involved in this affair, there isn't any story."

Anasette banged her mug on the countertop. "All right you guys, enough. Who's going to tell me what's happening downstairs?"

From the way the little jeweler was flipping her great, black mane around with quick jerks as she looked back and forth at the two males, she meant business. Usher launched into the story starting from when Anasette had vacated the car.

"What was all that shooting about?" injected Anasette, whose patience was wearing thin.

"Your landlord," said Szedlak, "was trying to blow this end of the city away with a canon."

"It was effective, wasn't it?" said Usher.

"Those guys weren't dumb enough to squat down and try to shoot under that door with you blazing away. Even if you missed, the shrapnel could have been deadly.

"Incidentally," said Szedlak, "don't forget to mention the passenger was waving his gun around as he tried to get out the car door. That was before you started blasting away."

"Two shots isn't blasting away," objected Usher.

"It is when you're using that heavy artillery."

"Knock it off," said Anasette. "Finish the story."

Szedlak picked up the ending of the story, but before he'd finished, his cell phone demanded attention. The lieutenant listened to a rather lengthy report. He said, "Tow it in and call forensics."

As Usher refilled the mugs, Szedlak said, "They found the hijacked car down in the Mexican barrio off of Santa Fe. It looks as if you were right about them being Hispanic."

Szedlak breezed through the rest of the story. Shoving his empty mug away, he said, "I have to get back to work and you have to start patching your garage door so that my car can go back out on patrol."

Usher went out to work with the plywood. He couldn't get the vehicles out to go down to the grocery store or restaurant, so Anasette ordered delivery pizza to the front door.

CHAPTER 10

Although Usher didn't have any pressing business away from the studio, it was acutely frustrating to have both his vehicles out of service behind the damaged door. The installation company would only give him a vague time when they might be able to get over and look at the damage.

Usher was left with either busywork or housecleaning.... neither prospect thrilled him. Anasette was working on a new commission, so she was no company.

At two o'clock the door guys showed up. Usher had them manipulate the wreckage enough so that he could get the Shelby and the van out. He did not want to leave his Mustang out in the weather, so he put it back inside and kept the van out.

While waiting on the work crew, Usher went down to his studio and turned on the lights. There was a hoard of little cleaning and maintenance jobs screaming for attention but he couldn't generate enough ambition to start them. The Nyla situation was occupying too much of his thought process.

When a call came in from an unidentified source in a California town that he didn't recognize, he was sufficiently out of sorts that, if it was a boiler room call, he would take pleasure in growling at the guy or gal.

"Hello."

"Orlop?"

"Kahn? What are you up to now?"

"Don't get nasty. I'm trying to do you another good turn."

"What?"

"Remember you were wondering why the Arnold woman had that stainless steel ball bearing in her hip pocket? While I was looking up something else, I came across a reported date-rape drug case where a stainless steel ball bearing, wrapped in a tissue, had been stuffed into the victim's vagina. I poked around and found another similar case. One was 18 months ago and the other was six months ago. Both were on the coast south of San Francisco.

"In neither case did the victim have any idea of who the guy was and they only vaguely remembered the event. Condoms were used and no other DNA was found."

"Interesting. Does that raise any possibilities as far as you're concerned?"

"Nothing," said Kahn. "Other than she might have gotten pregnant after being given a date rape drug by the ball bearing bastard."

"There could be all sorts of victims out there who didn't report it."

"Yeah, the police say a lot of date rapes are not reported."

"Why are you passing this information along to me?"

There was a slight delay in the answer. "I still have no idea why those thugs attacked me. The only thing I can think of is the Arnold case. If this was a rape and subsequent murder, then the murderer wouldn't want anyone snooping around. I'm not going to feel safe until that case is solved."

"You can probably relax a couple of days. I think your guys made a play for me last night."

"How?" said a wound up Kahn.

Usher related the events of the evening.

"Damn! I haven't seen anything of them since when we were in Petaluma. I was hoping they'd forgotten or the affair was not serious enough to come after me again. If they're still active, I will have to stay out of sight."

"Thanks for the info. I don't know if or how it fits in."

After they rang off, Usher checked the time. It was too early to interrupt Anasette. You wait until martini time before disturbing her concentration. The preceding night she'd been lamenting the fact that she had to eat pizza when what she really wanted was a New York strip smothered with mushrooms at Fahrenheit 451.

Armed with the new information concerning the date rapes Usher settled down in the den section of his bedroom/office to do some mental gymnastics. He reviewed all he knew about the case. He plugged in the information from Khan. The most likely scenario was Kahn's suggestion, and when Usher added the Rufino Sautto material, some interesting possibilities presented themselves.

When it became late enough to broach Anasette, Usher hit his mental save button to file the murder case away.

Usher tapped on the door before sticking his head in to yell, "Had a call from your favorite journalist and I have to see Maruca. I'll buy you dinner at Dos Amigos." Actually, Usher wouldn't be paying for the dinner because Maruca would never take his money.

There was a slight hesitation before Anasette yelled back, "I'll be up in 20 minutes for my martini."

Usher smiled. Curiosity won out over creativity. This didn't always happen. While Anasette was showering, Usher set out the martini makin's and changed clothes.

When Anasette came around the corner from the elevator, she was executing a complicated dance step. She had changed from her white robe into the basic layers of her composite exterior outfit. Without any visible effort she hopped onto her stool at the dining bar.

"What did that worm want?"

Usher shoved a martini to Anasette. "He called to pass some information on to me."

"Him?"

"He is still afraid to show his face in public. He's decided that the Arnold case is the source of his problems. If I can find the murderer, he'd be off the hook."

Usher related what Kahn had to say.

Instead of commenting on the new information, Anasette went straight to the second point. "Why do you have to see Maruca?"

"You'll have to wait for dinner for that." When he received an exaggerated pout, Usher said, "I'm looking for an unbiased reaction and not a considered response."

"Boy, you know how to be mean. You're going to leave me dangling in the wind until we get to Dos Amigos."

"And even then, I want to pick my time."

"Oh, you're absolutely horrid." Her curiosity was now fully engaged.

As they entered the Mexican restaurant, Usher took note of the customers. It was still early for the Mexican cena. Two tables were occupied. One group was eating while the others were waiting for their food.

Maruca spotted the pair. First, she ordered one of the girls to make a fresh pot of coffee, then she descended on the new arrivals with a full throated greeting, "Mis amigos. Where have you been? Have you forgotten poor Maruca?"

She gave each a big hug while maneuvering them toward the big, round table in the corner near the kitchen door.

"It's been so long," complained the shapely Mexican woman who could have been anywhere between 20 and 30.

"I've been out of town for a while," said Usher in defense.

Turning to Anasette, she said, "What's he been doing? He never tells me."

"He was just messing around with another murder."

"Ooooh," cooed Maruca. "Tell me all about it." Before she was ready to listen, she yelled "coffee, coffee." at the girl standing in front of the machine.

Usher watched the other waitress carry a crowded tray to the other group of diners. "Is Juan in the kitchen?"

"Yes."

"Do you suppose he could join us for a bit?"

Always the proprietress, Maruca checked the status of the dining room before saying "Sure." She bounced up to collect him. Usher and Anasette smiled at each other. Maruca had too much respect for her husband to yell at him. They knew Juan returned the courtesy.

Although Juan didn't really care to appear in the dining room in his cooking clothes, he came out to enthusiastically greet Anasette and Usher.

When all four were seated around the table, Usher asked Maruca, "Do you remember the last time we were in Dos Amigos?"

"Sure, you brought that little boy in to thank me. Is he all right?" said Maruca with alarm.

"Oh, yes. He's fine. Do you remember what you said to me when we were leaving?"

Maruca was thinking back, but she wasn't coming up with anything that would warrant the question.

Anasette was perplexed too.

"As we left with Rube, you said that if I came up with another, I shouldn't forget you."

Maruca smiled with the memory.

Do you suppose that you could handle a little girl about this long?" He held his hands out about 20 inches apart.

Anasette's eyes widened with understanding.

Both Maruca and Juan looked puzzled, so Usher continued. "This is just a preliminary inquiry to see if you would be interested in raising a few days old little girl as your own to adulthood?"

Now it was the Mexican couples turn to be amazed. Maruca started to say "yes," but clinched it off until she looked at Juan. Usher had never seen a more imploring look. Juan smiled at his wife and said, "Si."

Maruca added the translation "Yes," so the meaning wouldn't be lost.

Usher held up his hands. "Hold on, don't get too excited. This is the most preliminary inquiry. You must hear it all out and then come to a firm decision. Then work can begin to see if the baby is available and if custody can be obtained.

"At this moment, the whole proposition is just a figment of my imagination. So the chances of pulling this off are very remote but one has to start somewhere."

Usher paused while fresh coffee was served. "If you have followed the news in the last few days you heard about a baby."

"The dead mother," cried Maruca. "The poor girl....and pobre babé. That is the one?"

"Yes," said Usher. "As far as any of the doctors can tell, the baby is perfectly healthy, but there could be unseen complications from such a pregnancy." Usher briefly described the birth and what had happened to the baby. "The important thing is that at this moment, Nyla, has a guardian ad litem. Her fate hasn't been turned over to the juvenile services or the courts....Yet."

"Nyla?" said Anasette.

"Yes, the Tyrant's pet name."

"How do you get a little baby?" said Maruca, wanting to get back on target.

"I don't, but I looked into the matter on the request of somebody with a very distant blood interest, who has more money than years. He wants the child to have the benefits of growing up with a loving family instead of a foster home."

An agonized expression came over Maruca's face. "Those people will never let a former prostitute have a baby."

"That shouldn't enter into the discussion. The relative is the one who would be seeking custody. You'd be his employee, so to speak, tending the baby."

"And we're not gringos," said Juan.

"There is a possibility that the unknown father could be of Mexican origin."

Just then a couple with an infant came into the restaurant.

"Oh," said Maruca as she looked at the little bundle.

"So far," continued Usher, "No one has stepped forward to claim the child. There are hosts of people expressing an interest in adopting her, but people close to the affair feel that there is a high risk she'd be a trophy item to be exploited. They would rather that Nyla had a chance to grow up without the situation of her birth always present."

The waitress brought a ticket for the new arrivals. Juan looked uncomfortable. Maruca said, "Go. I will remember every word."

"If this were to happen," said Usher, "my friend would set aside money to handle any major expenses and to get Nyla launched on her own. You would have to take care of the day-by-day costs such as food, clothes, allowance, so forth."

"What about long-term legal status?" asked Anasette.

"No one has gotten that far along," said Usher, "but I would expect adoption would be the ultimate goal."

The waitress delivered a tray of tortilla chips and a bowl of Juan's special hot sauce, which was too picante to serve in a restaurant north of the border.

"Tell me about her," said Maruca with a wistful look.

"Don't get too anxious," warned Usher. "This is just an inquiry to find out if you are interested."

"Please."

"I don't know that much about her. I saw her born on closed-circuit TV. The doctor lifted a little red, wiggling thing above his head. The one thing I can say is that she has a fine set of lungs. Later, I saw a newspaper picture of her. It looked as if she had a wisp of dark hair."

"Ohhhhh," sighed Maruca.

Usher looked at Anasette. When they made eye contact, Usher nodded toward Maruca. Anasette slipped out of the booth and went around to slide into Maruca's side

Anasette was so much smaller, she just laid her head on Maruca shoulder. In a soft voice he said, "Dream, but don't start buying baby clothes and building a nursery. Usher is just seeing if you are interested. There are a lot of borders to cross."

A platter of empanadas arrived at the table. While Anasette was trying to bring the raging fires of expectation under control, Usher nibbled on chips.

More customers arrive. Juan would be chained to the stove. However, taking care of the new orders didn't get in the way of him keeping a constant flow of Mexican edibles from arriving at the round table.

After Anasette brought Maruca back down to earth, the consummate hostess started calling for plates and flatware.

While Usher and Anasette dined on a vast assortment of Mexican delicacies, Dos Amigos became a busy spot. Maruca was pressed into duty.

After the artists had eaten far too much, they waylaid Maruca long enough for Usher to say, "Talk this over with Juan. If you guys would be willing to give a little girl a loving home, be ready to tell me when I call. Will you be here at 2:00 o'clock in the afternoon?"

"We'll be here."

"I'll call you tomorrow."

On the way back to the van, Anasette hung onto Usher's arm and laid her head on his shoulder.

"Do you think you can pull it off?"

Usher didn't answer for a bit. "It's not me that has to do all of that hard work. It all depends on Jangala. At the moment, I think he's willing to do it, but I believe he's becoming aware of his mortality. It is hard to say which way he will go....either pour on the coal to get everything done that he can or decide to lie back and coast to the finish line.

"Jangala's history says he will continue to charge into the future even if it is on a pair of canes. A lot will depend on his health."

Anasette commented, "I don't recall ever seeing such desire in anyone's eyes as when she realized what you were asking. If it can't be done, Maruca will go through the same agony as a new mother having her firstborn die of SIDS."

"That's why I'm here. I saw a touch of it when we brought Rube by. Before I try to get an infant, I have to be absolutely certain I have a good home waiting. There could always be something going on unbeknownst to us."

Anasette snorted, "Like Juan playing around?"

"No, but a doctor could have told Maruca yesterday that she had pancreatic cancer."

As they climbed into the cold van, Anasette said, "What are you going to do now?"

"I'll have to sell Maruca and Juan to Jangala. I don't know how he feels about Mexicans. That may or may not have any influence."

"You told Maruca that the father might be Mexican. You're thinking of the judge's son?"

"He seems to be the logical choice. There are just too many coincidences. I would suggest that Alecia was a rape victim and recognized the rapist in the newspaper article. We're the only ones that know about that article that's the link."

"The police are not going to take too kindly to you having that article." said Anasette.

"No, they might get downright twitchy."

"I'll ask the same question. What are you going to do now? Are you going after Sautto?"

"I'd like to ignore the murder part and concentrate on getting Nyla and Maruca hooked up, but I still have the problem of those thugs. I'm pretty certain they weren't bill collectors. The murder and those guys have to be linked."

When Usher approached his studio building, he drove around the block. "Watch for any exhaust signs. It's too cold to stake out a place without some heat. Those guys didn't appear to be dressed for a Colorado winter." He made a dry run down the alley before returning to pull into the driveway in front of the garage door

The garage door installers were still there but they were winding up a long day. A guy came over to explain why they hadn't finished. "They don't make doors like your old one anymore. The fittings in the closer mounts are different. In the morning, we'll make new brackets at the shop and then install them about mid morning. You can't use the door yet, but the building is secure."

"Stick with me until I check all the doors to make sure we have no visitors."

Anasette had no objection to a security delay. Twice bad guys had tried to do her harm in that building.

They made the rounds checking each first floor lock. Since

Usher had turned off the electricity to the elevator, it hadn't been used. Ultimately, they ended up in overstuffed chairs in the gallery with glasses of Presidente Brandy in hand to top off a bountiful Mexican meal.

Anasette had made a detour into Usher's bedroom to turn on the electric blanket and shed a few outer layers. Now that no Hispanic gunmen were threatening her and she was warming up inside and out, she had time to consider the future. "How are you going to sell Yrlo on this scheme?"

"Yrlo?"

"Oh, yes, when you were in California, we had occasion to speak any number of times. He isn't as ferocious as reputed. Of course, age may have something to do with that." Anasette smiled sweetly.

Usher shook his head. The Little Tyrant wasn't the first old firebrand that Anasette had charmed.

"Before I go any further, I'd better check with Sasha Khan to see if the baby has developed any problems. I'd hate to foist a defective baby off on Maruca."

Anasette shifted her body a little further sideways in the chair so she could look directly at Usher without having to turn her head.

"Men," said Anasette in a very unappreciative tone.

"Men, what?"

"No matter what condition that baby is in, she would be one of the most loved babies on earth. If she died at age 3, it would be a great loss to Maruca, but she would have rather suffered through that than never to have had a baby at all.

"Men want little or nothing to do with damaged goods. However, women can wrap a flawed child in a very warm blanket of love. Get that baby for Maruca."

Usher sat for a considerable time looking into the dark eyes that had him pinned to the chair. Ultimately, he said nothing.... just nodded.

Seldom was one at a loss to know how Anasette felt about any given subject. However, most of the time, she didn't use that many words to make her point known.

Usher changed the subject. "Jangala expressed concern that time was short and that he would like contact with Jon and Eric. Do you want to run out to the farm tomorrow evening? I need to talk with Britta. I want to keep Jangala active and involved. He has too many projects going to fade out on us now."

Chapter 11

The day had been one that Usher would like to forget. He garage door finally was finished. And then he had the insurance adjuster argument.

Usher had called ahead to the farm. He had turned down an invitation to dinner. The plan was to arrive just as the colonels returned to the bunkhouse, as they called it. Jon and Eric would be given the dishwashing duties and Anasette would keep them from eavesdropping, as was their normal bent. After talking with Britta, Usher and Anasette were to stop by for a drink with the colonels.

Finally, the day of the irritations passed. At 5:30 Usher collected Anasette. It was almost dark when the Shelby Mustang backed out of the parking area. They were headed for a funky little diner about three blocks away. Both artists enjoyed the offbeat spot for an occasional change. There was always something on the menu that was seldom found elsewhere.

Usher checked the rear view here and found nothing disturbing.

At the diner, they were met by a comforting blast of hot air carrying a riot of savory smells. There was little separation between the kitchen and dining room.

Anasette turned her nose up to Usher's kidney stew, preferring the stuffed bell pepper. They passed on dessert, because with any forewarning, Britta would bake a rhubarb or gooseberry pie for Usher. She always kept the frozen makings on hand.

As they passed out of the city to the east, Usher started to pay more attention to his rearview mirror. "I think we have company."

Usher handed Anasette his cell phone. "I'm going to pull up to the next convenience store. You jump out and go inside. Buy a couple bottles of water or iced tea, whatever. If they try to make a move, call cavalry. If I leave I'll just drive around the block. When Usher pulled off the street, he didn't nose into the parking slot but parked along the curb near the gasoline pumps.

The car behind pulled off to the side of the street. When Anasette crawled back into the car and Usher headed out, the tailing car followed.

"Why are they following us? Do they expect us to lead them somewhere? said Anasette.

"No, I think they are probably trying to find someplace where we'll be alone. They weren't successful getting into the studio. Now that they know that I am armed, they won't try getting into there again. They're probably hoping that we'll give them an opening."

"Like what?"

"At Fahrenheit 451, there is a large, secluded parking lot. If we'd gone there, they might have had an opportunity."

"What are you going to do?"

"Call Britta. The colonels should still be at the dinner table. I'd like to talk to Colonel McClintock."

Anasette found a number in memory and punched it in. "Hi, Britta. We're headed in your direction. Is Colonel McClintock still there? Usher would like to talk to him." Anasette passed the phone back.

"Hi Colonel, what have you and the boys been done lately to keep life interesting?"

"Not a da......darn thing," was the gruff replied. "Got anything in mind?"

"Maybe. At the moment, we're just about to leave the city and I have a tail. It is probably the two young thugs that tried to jump me in California and ruined my garage door a couple of nights ago when they tried to get in."

"Oh, really," said the colonel with heightened interest.

"Would you guys like to have a little fun tonight?"

"You bet." Usher could hear an excited babble begin in the background. "We're about 20 minutes out. Better cut that to 15. We'll be coming in fast. Get Britta and the kids into the dressage ring. If they follow me in, I'll drive right into the ring. When they hit the yard, turn on the floods and courteously asked them to get out of their car." McClellan snorted in his ear. "Be careful, these guys are probably armed, but I don't know how dedicated they are to whatever cause they have. I don't know what their beef is. I just may let you guys find that out."

"That sounds like a plan to me. We'll be ready before you can get here." McClellan broke the connection.

"It could get a little rough," said Anasette. "How about Britta and the kids?"

"You don't have to worry about them. Do you think that those old war horses would ever let any harm come to them?"

"A real honest-to-gosh gun fight....exactly like on Saturday morning TV."

"I'm not worried about those boys. All three have been through worse."

Usher had been keeping his eye on their tail. They were pretty good. They varied the distance and occasionally changed lanes. They took advantage of other traffic and changed their patterns.

"When we leave the state road onto the county road, I'm going to turn up the speed if they follow me. It will probably evolve into a race. It is so secluded out here, anyplace would probably suit them. I'm going to lead them to believe that I spotted them when we make the turn and I'm trying to outrun them. I want them to think I can't shake them on a paved road so I'll try losing them on a gravel road."

"Be careful. Out here there's still snow and ice."

"Right."

As soon as the tail followed the Mustang onto the state road, Usher accelerated sharply. He had to be careful. That Shelby could outrun a stock car anytime. Two sets of headlights when streaking off into the distance. The sparse traffic presented no problems. Anasette looked at the grin on Usher's face as she hung onto anything substantial. "You're loving this," she said accusingly.

Usher let his pursuers get a little closer. Then he suddenly braked and slid sideways as he abandoned the blacktop and darted down a gravel road into the darkness.

Coming out of the turn, Usher gave the appearance of fishtailing. The pursuing car made the turn. Usher straightened out and plunged down what was a very long driveway to a cluster of dark farm buildings. The bad guys were committed before any building appeared in their headlights.

The Mustang continued past the farmhouse. The brake lights came on as the side of a gigantic barn appeared. It seemed like the chase was about to end.

Then the prey disappeared behind a wall of dazzling white lights. The driver was blinded. As he braked sharply, a magnified voice barked, "Come out of the car with your hands in sight. No guns."

As soon as the driver brought the car to a halt, automatic weapon fire disrupted two stripes on the ground right in front of the car.

"Out or we'll blow you out," came an emphatic command.

Both front doors flew open revealing two sets of empty hands. Carefully, two young men dressed in jeans, heavy black coats and black sneakers stepped out.

Usher had driven into the dressage ring, but both he and Anasette quickly exited the car and were peering out the door at the evolving events. Two of the colonels had the pair of thugs draped over the hood of their car until they were patted down for weapons and ID.

Colonel McClintock sidled up along the barn. "Hi, Usher, Anasette. Just a minute, while I get Britta and the kids. Then I'll escort you all back to the house. The boys and I will use the ring when we talk to those jokers. We'll find out what they're after."

McClintock disappeared into the darkness toward one of the RVs, which showed little slits of light around the shaded windows.

Shortly, the colonel was back with Britta and the three boys. "No talking. Follow me." McClintock led the way around the garden area to the back entry.

In the house, Usher waited until the two thugs had been marched into the barn before turning on the lights. With the lights came a flood of questions. Britta had had the foresight to make a pot of coffee as soon as she knew Usher was en route. She poured drinks for everyone as the boys juggled chairs up to the big table.

With wide-eyed Jon, Eric and Ali present, Usher gave a sanitized version of the events leading up to the explosive episode that had just taken place in their yard. He didn't bring Jangala's name into the tale.

Usher kept waiting for word from the colonels. Finally, McClintock and Polanski came in for a cup of coffee and to warm up. An old fashioned wood cook stove was still part of the big, farm kitchen. In winter, Britta used it as addition to the house heating system.

McClintock remarked, "It's 16° out there."

"Did you find out what you have?" said Usher.

"Oh, yeah," said the colonel, as if it was a fore drawn conclusion that they'd get the information. "First off, they are Mexicans from Matamoros. They work for one of the big drug cartels. It took a little time, because their English leaves a lot to be desired. As far as we can figure, their boss sent them to California to help with a problem of one of their lesser bosses of the cartel."

"What?" said Usher.

McClintock referred to his little stack of 3 x 5 cards. "Rico."

"I wonder if that's for Rufino," said Usher.

The colonel shrugged his shoulders. "They don't know too much about any history. Rico tells them to do something and they do it."

"That cartel connection was hard to get out of them. When they realized they've been taken by four old duffers, they started to muscle up to try something. We didn't have any handcuffs or any of those plastic wristbands, so we had to improvise."

Anasette raised her eyebrows.

McClintock chuckled. "We had an 8-foot length of heavy logging chain and a couple of padlocks with long shackles. We just chained them together by something a couple of young Mexican machos don't want to lose." The adults around the table just about croaked. The boys looked perplexed.

"Anyway, we got them controlled but they still weren't talking, so we took their clothes and left them chained in the middle of the dressage ring. We went into the RV with its heater until they decided to give us what we wanted."

"How come they're trying to get us?" said Usher

"They were told to find out why you are interested in a baby in California. Who are you working for?"

"What were they supposed to do to Kahn?"

"Kahn. We didn't ask about anyone by that name."

"Do you suppose they are still in a talkative mood?" said Usher.

"I imagine so. If not, we'll just tie them outside until they get that way."

Usher reached for his jacket. Anasette did too. When Usher tried to say something, the jeweler said, "I was there too when they tried to get into the studio."

When Usher and Anasette crowded into the RV, two pathetic looking naked creatures were sitting side by side on a small couch. They were scrunched up as much as possible with their arms clamped at their sides and their hands clasping their crotches, trying to conserve as much heat as possible.

Their agony was compounded when they realized one of the new arrivals was a girl....especially one who started snickering as her eyes traced the logging chain.

"From here on out, every time I hear that comment about rattling one's chain, this is the image that will come to mind," said Anasette.

Usher greeted the other colonels. After a brief exchange, Usher turned to the two Mexicans. "Why were you after Kalib Khan?"

Neither made any pretense of answering Usher's question. The silence continued until McClintock reached down to grab the loop of chain lying on the floor between the two prisoners.

"No," cried the smaller of the two. "Jefe told us to."

"What did your jefe tell you to do?"

Neither answered until McClintock started shaking the chain. Both men had to relinquish their crotch holds to grab the chain preventing any jerks or weight shifts from getting past their hands.

"Jefe say, 'Kill him'."

"Were you supposed to kill me too?"

"No."

"Is Rico, Rufino Sautto?"

That question scared both young toughs badly.

"I think you just asked a question that could get both of these punks killed," said McClintock.

McClintock dropped the chain. "What do you want to do with these bluebirds?"

"Hang on to them a few minutes while I check with Szedlak. Take all the stuff out of their pockets and let them dress but leave them chained up.

Colonel Golden squeezed into the RV with a cardboard box. "Here are all the toys they left in the car. They had a fine assortment of arms....two 9 mm, a .22 and an Uzzi. There also ticket stubs. If they flew in yesterday, they must have good friends to get this kind of firepower."

"Shall we ask them about that?" inquired McClintock.

"Ah, let's leave something for Szedlak to do," said Usher. "I'll be back in a few minutes."

Usher left Anasette to tell Britta and the kids what was going on. He went into the living room to call Lieutenant Szedlak in Denver. Fortunately, he had just arrived at the office, so he didn't have to interrupt some other assignment.

"What's happening, Orlop? Need another garage door?"

"No, I'm not in the studio. I'm out at the farm and those two guys chased us until we caught them."

"You mean you led them into an ambush. Anyone survive?"

"Oh, they're in good shape. I have two young Mexican nationals, armed to the teeth, even though they just flew in from California. They are trying to kill Kahn and try to find out who I work for. It appears that this ties in with the Alecia Arnold murder. Do you want 'em?"

"Sure, I want them, but that sheriff out there is going to have a cow if I show up."

"I imagine I could prevail on the colonels to play UPS and deliver them to you. Of course, if one of the colonels drives their car it will mess up evidence."

"That car wasn't involved in anything but tailing you. Yeah, bring them in."

When Usher passed the word, there was a flurry of activity. The BARs disappeared to be replaced with Army .45 semi-automatic handguns. A van with all of its seats was brought around. The duties were divided up. McClintock would drive the van with Stoner riding shotgun. Polanski was to drive the rental car. Since his hip was acting up, Golden volunteered to stay to keep the farm safe. As the van and the car pulled out of the yard, Golden had a self-satisfied grin on his face. He didn't even limp while walking into the house.

"You big old fraud," said a laughing Anasette.

Golden smiled. "Why should I go wandering around the countryside on a frigid night like this when I can play great warrior to the little boys who will be clamoring for my story until their mother chases them off to bed with a ball bat? I'll hear everything that happens in Denver at least a dozen times and I won't risk having to change a flat tire."

Usher and Anasette retrieved the Shelby Mustang from the dressage ring and caught up with the lead cars. The delivery of the two prisoners to the downtown police facility caused a sensation. Szedlak was hanging around waiting for the posse. The two Mexicans were marched into the front door with coils of shiny logging chain being carried by the prisoners and the ends disappearing into their flies. It struck everyone's funny bone.

As soon as Szedlak saw the situation, he whisked the prisoners into a room. A few minutes later he reappeared with his hand stuck out, palm up. He looked at Usher, who said, "Not me."

Anasette smiled brightly, "Not me."

McClintock was digging around in his pants pockets. Finally, he produced a key and ceremoniously dropped it into the lieutenant's hand.

Szedlak had another officer take Usher and his entourage to the lieutenant's office. He stormed into the office a few minutes later. "What are you trying to do to me? The captain is on my back already. In the morning, the chief will be there too. Photos of those guys are already on YouTube after you paraded them into the waiting room. The camera phones were busy too. Not a lick of work is being done and I'll get the blame for all the overtime the department will have to pay."

Szedlak flopped down in his chair. He could see that he was getting no sympathy from the crowd, so he said, "Whatcha'got?"

Between the five-some, they gave Szedlak pretty much the whole story. Usher had to dance around a bit by not making the connection between Rufino Sautto and the Supreme Court. He wanted to play with that lead himself.

"Oh, yes," said Colonel McClintock, "here's the keys to that rental car. It's in the lot outside. The guns are in the trunk. None of our prints are on them."

"Is the car full of automatic weapon holes?" asked Szedlak.

McClintock indignantly retorted, "Of course not. How would something like that ever happen?"

Szedlak didn't press the issue. He called forensic to handle the car and contents. It was close to midnight before they were able to finish at the police station. The colonels headed back to the farm. Usher and Anasette returned to the studio with a whole rhubarb pie that Britta passed to them as they left. It had been overlooked in all of the excitement.

"In the morning, I have to talk with Britta about Jangala. Later in the day, I must get busy trying to get Maruca her baby. I want to be armed with a plan that lets Jangala get closer to the boys. I'd rather he had something else to worry about other than his mortality. The boys will be home tomorrow. How about running interference while I talk to their mother?"

"Sure, that's fun."

As soon as the Mustang turned off the county road, Ali appeared on the back porch. Jon and Eric quickly followed. The dash began to beat the car to the cattle guard into the yard. Usher accelerated and so did the boys. It turned out to be a draw again. The kids gamboled about the car like frisky colts until Usher brought it to a stop by the kitchen door.

Jon and Eric waited on the driver's side so they could walk arm in arm with Usher to the house. Before Ali was on the scene, their mother had corrected their manners so that Anasette would also have an escort. Ali had a deep attraction to Anasette and he was proud to be her escort.

Britta was bustling around the kitchen getting the coffee set up and juice for the boys. The immediate item of conversation surrounded the prior night's activities. Everyone knew what went down at the farm but they had little understanding of what led up to the affair. They also wanted a report on what happened at the police station.

While Anasette was describing the event with the bad guys and the studio garage door, Usher asked Britta if he could have a word with her and bobbed his head toward the front room, which was out of sight from the kitchen.

Britta settled down in her chair which was at the end of the davenport where the boys sat to watch TV....if they weren't on the floor. Usher perched on the couch.

"The other day I was in Portland at Jangala's on another matter. You and the boys came up. Don't worry. There's nothing wrong. I think Jangala is worried about his mortality. He is afraid he will die before he has a chance to meet the boys. They are so young and he feels so old. He's afraid the twain shall never meet. He doesn't want to meddle in anything. If I am correct, Jangala is one of the most astute judges of character and ability around. And before he checks out, he needs to know that he made sure he has the proper people in the proper place so that the Jangala Empire can endure. Soon he will need to assess the boys."

"It's been less than two years..."

"It's not a very long time in our lives but it is a big chunk of theirs. Anyway I'm not suggesting anything but an introduction of Jangala's name in a different context. In the car I have two copies of Lyyli's book that are autographed for the boys. How about giving them the books? If I'm not mistaken they'll devour that book. You will then probably have to field a bunch of questions."

"They know Lyyli was working on a book. You are right, they'll inhale all of the words right off the page."

"Let's give the boys the books and see how they react. You'll be able to tell by the type of interest they show."

"Will that be enough for Mr. Jangala?"

Usher made a little face. "I think so....At least for the time being. If not, we'll have to think of something else."

Britta and Usher returned to the kitchen. The boys were looking very expectant. They knew that when Usher and their mother had a private conversation they were somehow involved.

"There's a brown paper wrapped package in the back of the Mustang," said Usher. Will one of you boys go get it for me?"

The kitchen was voided of boys so fast that it was like they had been flushed out of the back door.

All of the adults laughed. Anasette started to say something but before she could get anything out, the boys were back. Eric was the proud bearer of the package.

To sidestep any sibling rivalry over who would get to open the package, Usher directed that it be given to Anasette.

Anasette ripped the paper off and slipped a book to Jon and Eric, with the comment, "Lyyli thanks you each with an autographed copy of her new book."

There were a couple of "wows" before both boys seemed to disappear between the covers. Ali was suddenly abandoned and a forlorn look slipped across his face.

Britta reached out to scoop Ali into her arms. In a conspiratorial whisper, she said, "While the guys are occupied, would you go to see if Colonel Golden would be willing to take you to the store and buy a big pack of corn tortillas? We are having carnitas tonight, but I need fresh tortillas."

Ali enthusiastically bobbed his head as he quietly slipped out of the room. Before he could get out the back door, Britta had to remind him to put on his jacket.

Both Usher and Anasette watched the interplay. The older boys may have been engrossed in their books but they still hadn't missed Ali's errand.

On the drive home, Anasette was chuckling over the antics of the kids. "Just after you guys went into the living room, Jon suddenly had to go to the bathroom. He headed for the upstairs bath, so he could go through the living room. I had to remind him that he could use the one off the porch. All three were trying to be quiet enough to pick up any hint of what was going on. Jon and Eric have trained Ali well.

"How do you come out with Britta?"

"We'll wait to see what questions come out of the books. I think Jangala will view this as progress."

Chapter 12

Usher put the phone back on the base. Actually, he'd expected the call to Jangala to be a much more prolonged affair. The Little Tyrant listened to Usher's presentation. He asked a few questions to gain more information, but there was no questioning of Usher's proposal. Usher had expected some hesitancy when he gave Maruca's history and qualifications as a suitable parent for baby Nyla. There had been none.

Jangala was pleased that Jon and Eric were reading Lyyli's book.

Now all Usher had to do was to email all the pertinent facts on Maruca and Juan. The attorneys were already working on the custody papers. For the moment, there was nothing more he could do on the baby affair. Usher's mind wandered back to the Sauttos. With the information in his possession, he felt that the chances were pretty good that Rufino was Alecia's murderer. At least, he should be thoroughly investigated, but Usher also realized that the chances of the local authorities conducting any meaningful inquiry were remote.

Sauttos had too much wealth and political power. Someone in this case had already provided a substantial demonstration with the records tampering and a complete computer failure. Now, there was the possible cartel connection.

Usher had no intention of getting involved in a murder investigation half a continent away, but he also felt that his information should be used in an attempt to right a wrong.

Usher watched his cold coffee swirl around in the stainless steel sink. Stainless. His eyes followed the coffee as it drained away except in a tiny dimple that he had made when he dropped a cast-iron pot into the sink. That little dimple reminded Usher of the dimples in the jewelry case he'd found in Alecia's apartment.

Usher poured himself more coffee before returning to his office area in the bedroom. He was mentally reviewing Alecia's room. One item was missing....a phone.

After getting home from California, Usher had dumped all of his notes and bits of paper into a manila envelope. He shuffled through the residue until he came up with the name of the cat lady. Caller information produced a number, and dialing produced a response.

"Milli. This is Usher Orlop, the guy who was asking about Alecia Arnold. You showed me her hidy-hole."

"Oh yes, I remember you."

"How have you and Sir Lawrence been?"

With the mention of her cat by name, Usher sensed a warming.

"We're both fine. The vet tells me I should cut down on his meals."

"Millie. What I called about is that I don't remember a phone in Alecia's room. Did the police take it or didn't Alecia have one?"

"She couldn't afford a phone. I let her use mine occasionally."

"For long distance calls?"

"If necessary."

"How did you take care of the charges?"

"She asked for the charges and dropped the money into a ceramic cat above the phone." There was the sound of coins rattling. "There's money in there, but I can't remember when the calls were made.

"Could you please check and see whether or not Alecia made any long distance calls in the last two weeks that she was with us?"

"I just got the bill. I haven't paid it yet. One moment."

There was a general rustling around and the sound of an envelope being torn open. After a short silence, Millie came back online.

"Yes, there were two calls I don't recognize." She read off two numbers and the dates of the calls. "Both are California numbers, but I don't know where."

"I can find out. Thanks so much. We still don't know who killed Alecia. Maybe these phone numbers will help. Thank you, Millie. You take good care of Sir Lawrence, you hear?"

Milli laughed. "Don't worry about that."

Usher went through a reverse directory and found that one number was for Manuel Sautto. The only thing he could find out about the second number was that it was a cell phone.

With the addition of the Sautto call four days before the murder, Usher ranked the probability that young Sautto either killed Alecia, or had it done, very high. Of course, there was an off chance that it could've been a random act or an act of opportunity by someone else before she met Sautto.

The probability continued to rise as various little pieces fell into place. In Usher's mind, he was guilty until proven otherwise. The remaining problem was what to do with this supposition.

He could turn the information over to Szedlak, but the lieutenant would just have to pass it along and it would probably fall into a black hole just as fast as if Usher had called it in personally.

As far as he could see, the only possibility of getting any action would be to get a conservative politician of sufficient strength who would want to block Sautto from the Supreme Court. The problem was he didn't know anything about California or Washington DC politicians. And something would have to be done soon, before Sautto was confirmed.

Further thought was put on hold when Szedlak called. "I don't know what's going on. Your two Mexican boys have just had a court appearance on the attempted entry into your place. They're not asking for bail. They don't want to leave the jail. I think they're afraid they'll get killed. Do you have any explanation for that?"

"No reason I know of, unless their jefe feels that their failures rate a death sentence. They missed the mark three times."

"It looks as if they'd rather do jail time and be deported. I'm going home to bed. Go take a nap so you don't get into any more trouble. I always get the call."

When Usher hung up the phone, he debated with himself as to whether or not to call Kahn to let them know about the Mexicans. He rejected the idea since he didn't want to spend his time chasing the reporter down.

Suddenly, Usher stopped that consideration for a new one. He swiveled around so the snow-clad Rockies could form a canvas for another line of thought.

It didn't take him long to come to a conclusion. He swung back around so he could check his caller ID for that unknown town in California.

"Whatcha want Orlop?"

"My, aren't we in a foul humor today."

"I'm tired of watching my back trail."

"You don't have to worry about the two Mexican boys. They're in the Denver jail and for some reason they don't want to leave."

"What have you got on them?"

"I don't know what the final charges will be, but they tried an armed entry into my studio. They are illegals and there are some weapons charges that could be used. Go on YouTube and look up 'chain gang'."

"Oh, I've heard about that. Several people have told me about them. They're the ones?"

"Yes, they admitted to my people that their jefe wanted you dead for some reason unknown to them."

"Unknown?"

"Those guys are just worker bees doing what they're told to do.

They don't have to know why, but I do."

There was silence on the other end of the phone before Kahn said, "What do you want?"

"I'm about to offer you the trade of your lifetime."

A suspicious "Yes?" came back along to the earpiece.

"I'll give you the political story of your life in exchange for an agreement that you and your minions will ignore me and any of my interests from here on out."

"Since when have you ever been willing to take my word for anything?"

"Oh, I realize I'm taking a chance. But, my people can keep your head on a swivel watching your back for a long, long time. And also you will probably find it in your own best interests to stay on my good side."

"Okay, providing your story is as you advertise."

"The murderer of Alecia Arnold is Rufino Sautto."

"Who?"

"Rufino Sautto, son of Manuel Sautto." There was silence on the other end.

"Judge Manuel Sautto."

"WHAT?"

"That's right, the Supreme Court nominee. I'm giving you the name, but you'll have to do something with it. Don't you think that is a story worthy of your talents?"

"It is, if you're not setting me up. How'd you come up with this name?"

Usher began to piece the picture together while reserving the source of a lot of information. When he had built his case, Usher said, "With that amount of information, don't you think it warrants further inquiry?"

"Yes, but why don't you be the hero and take this to the police?"

Usher laughed. "What do you think would happen to this supposition if it were taken to any jurisdictions in that area? Someone has already screwed up the whole computer system and state files.

"Suppose you're right. If nothing else, this could be dragged out for months or years. And Sautto could be approved in a month or less to a lifetime term. He's in Washington now glad-handing Senators.

"If you pull this one off, your name could be up there with the elite of the investigative reporters."

"Of course, there's also a chance of getting killed," said Kahn.

When Usher hung up, he was left with an empty feeling. He had just passed all that work onto someone else. To be unneeded was foreign territory. There wasn't even an active project on the bench in the studio.

The only unfinished item of business was to tell Anasette about siccing Kahn onto the Sauttos. She wouldn't care for it because Kalib Kahn was either at the top or at least well up on her crud list. She bought "The Orbiter" every week so Kahn's articles could reinforce her dislike for him.

Usher stomped on the floor over Anasette's apartment before dialing her. She had a propensity to ignore the phone when engrossed in one of her projects. If she was in a creative mode she could still ignore the phone after the stomp.

"My landlord calls...."

"When it's late enough for a martini, come up and I'll tell you about today's flights of fancy. And then I'll take you to Fahrenheit 451 for dinner."

"You're on." Anasette hung up.

Usher knew she'd be late enough so that the hors d'oeuvre bar would be gone by the time they arrived at the restaurant. He'd use the time to clear away a backlog of paperwork. When he heard the shower come on, he'd have sufficient time to ready himself.

The two artists moved their martinis into the gallery. Anasette curled up in a large chair. "What flights of fancy did you take today? You were to talk to Jangala also."

"Yeah, I called as early as I thought he'd be up and moving. I presented my pitch for Maruca and I didn't receive much of the grilling I had expected. In the past I really had to sell my proposals. This time I wasn't dangling any incentives in front of him and he seemed to accept what I proposed without any provisions.

"You were worried he might be thinking about his mortality. You think that was it?"

"I don't know. In any case, the attorneys are working on it now."

"What other fanciful flights did you take today?"

"Oh, you'll love or hate this one."

Anasette was about to hold her martini glass up for a refill. Instead she set it down on the chair. Her curiosity was aroused.

"I called your favorite journalist."

"Kahn? To tell him about the Mexicans?"

"Oh, that, and I gave him the name of Alecia's killer."

"You did what?"

"You heard me. I wasn't as far out on a limb as you think. I made a connection between them." Usher proceeded to tell Anasette about talking to the cat lady and Alecia's phone calls.

"Why did you give such a huge story to him of all people?"

"I can't do anything from here with no resources. Neither can Szedlak. If I pass the word to the local authorities, I bet it would disappear and I might even have someone on my back again.

"Kahn is already involved and he has the capability of trying it in the court of public opinion even if he can't get the authorities to look into it."

"It sounds as if this might be too dangerous. You've seen what a coward he is."

"You're right. He's a real physical coward. That's probably why he is so slimy. He gets what he wants from the shadows without physical confrontation."

"Is this going to affect the baby's proceedings?" said Anasette as she held up her glass for a refill.

As Usher moved to comply with Anasette's request, he continued his plot at a higher volume.

"One concern I've had is that Jangala's name is going to appear on legal papers in San Jose County. He has to establish his relationship to Nyla to make this work. Kahn would probably poke around in any legal filing and he'd probably recognize the Jangala name. The old man doesn't want that."

By the time Anasette was stuffed full of New York strip and mushrooms, she acceded to the proposition that Usher's scheme might have some merit. However, nothing could convince her that Kahn would lay off harassing them if the opportunity arose.

Despite whatever misgivings she was still harboring concerning Usher's alliance with Kahn, Anasette snapped on the electric blanket when they returned to the studio.

It was still dark outside when Usher's phone rang. He never liked odd hour calls, so he rolled over to turn on the bedside lamp so he could read the caller ID. It took him a moment to recognize Kahn's cell phone address.

Anasette roused up enough to give a groggy, "Who's that?"

Before Usher reacted, the answering machine picked up the call.

During the machine recording, Usher said "Kahn." He moved to the desk for the speaker phone.

"Orlop, pick up. Come on Orlop...."

"It's the middle of the night, Kahn."

"You are right, you nailed him."

Kahn was so excited he was hyperventilating.

"Kahn, are you driving?"

"Sautto's the killer."

"Kahn. Pull off the road and tell me what you're talking about."

There was a squall of tires.

"Kahn?"

"It's all right. I just had to brake to pull into a parking lot."

"Good. Turn off the engine, sit back, take a deep breath and tell me what you're talking about."

"You'll never believe this. I don't believe this. When you called I was in Frisco. I drove down to Carmel. I arrived in the late afternoon. I found the Sautto home. As I was driving around the block, I noticed that there was what appeared to be an apartment under the garage of the main house. The apartment has its own garage and carport. As I was driving by, a navy blue van was pulling out of the garage. Down the street I found a spot where I could watch the apartment. The guy working the van was Rufino Sautto. I looked him up before I left Frisco.

"I watched for a couple of hours while he cleaned and provisioned the van. He vacuumed inside and wiped down all surfaces. Then he put in an ice chest and stocked it with various import beers.

"After he finished with the van, he locked it up and crawled into a snazzy little BMW and headed for one of the better restaurants in town. I tailed him there and then ducked out to get a supply of fast food.

"Anyway, I stuck with him when he went home. At 11:00 pm he came out of the apartment dressed in casual beach clothes. He drove off in the van and I followed. We ended up at a house on the beach in Pacific Grove, where a big young people's party was in full swing. He parked down the street. When he left the van, he had two bottles of beer in hand. I followed along. Sautto hung back on the fringe of the party that was in the backyard of a fancy home. The party was spilling out onto the beach. There were those manufactured fire pits spotted all around. Sautto watch the activities for some time. Suddenly, he stepped up to a girl and offered her a beer. Apparently, she accepted. He twisted the caps off the beers and appeared to offer a toast. They clinked bottles and both took swigs. Then Sautto must have suggested that they dance. Sautto set his bottle on the edge of the garden planter and set the girl's bottle in a niche. While they were taking off their shoes to dance barefoot, Sautto switched bottles."

"You actually saw him switch the bottles?" said Usher.

"Yep. He was real smooth. They went over to a concrete pad where many couples were dancing. I pulled my cap down and sauntered by the planter and swapped the bottles back."

Kahn started to giggle. Through his giggles, he said, "I really did it.

"They danced up a storm. When they were all hot and breathless they ran back and grabbed their beers and took long drinks.

"When they finished their beers, Sautto motioned toward his van. He took the empties and it looked as if he was going for another round." Kahn started giggling again.

To get him off his giggle fest, Usher said, "Boy, that was a bold move."

Kahn remembered somebody else was listening. He sobered up and continued his story.

"As Sautto headed back toward the street, he motioned for the girl to come along. She hung back on the lawn saying she didn't want to walk on the blacktop.

"Sautto started to stagger. The girl became alarmed and called to ask what was wrong. That's when I stepped out." Kahn sounded very pleased with himself.

"I stepped past the girl saying, 'Mr. Moriarty is subject to occasional seizures. That's why he hires me to take him home.' I put his arm over my shoulder and said, 'Come on Mr. Moriarty, it's time to go."

"I walked across to his van, pulled the keys out of his pocket, opened the side door and dumped him in. By this time Sautto was completely out of it. As I went around to the driver's side, I could see that the girl had already returned to the party. Since no one was watching, I detoured to my car for my traveling kit. Before getting into the van, I put on rubber gloves from the kit.

"Then I had to find a place where we wouldn't be discovered. No one was home at the Sautto place and the van belonged there. We shouldn't be bothered. I parked the van in the carport. Behind the front seat is a light-proof curtain. There are lights in the back."

Anasette quietly crawled out of bed and picked up a robe for each of them from the closet. The furnace was still set on its nighttime setting. Clothed, they could migrate to the coffee pot while Kahn talked on.

"On the trip back to the Sautto house, I figured out what I'd do. I stripped him bare-ass naked and using those plastic bands the police use for handcuffs that I found in the Sautto's goody-box or kit. I cuffed his hands behind him and his feet together.

"I found a supply of stainless steel ball bearings in that kit, so I wrapped one in a tissue and stuffed it up his ass."

Anasette had to stifle an exclamation. Her broad grin indicated she felt that Kahn had done something right for a change.

"Whatever drug he was trying to slip to that chick really works fast."

"Did you see him administer it?" said Usher.

"I watched, but it was very little light and I was quite a ways away. I didn't see him put it in his bottle, but I had noticed he turned slightly away from the girl when he set his bottle on the wall.

"I'm glad I recorded the whole thing. His speech was quite slurred and sometimes he spoke in Spanish. I was having a hard time getting anything out of him. About three hours later I could see he was beginning to come out of it. So I slipped him a little C-117."

"What's C-117?" said Usher.

"Oh, that's the truth serum the Soviet intelligence used. Actually, truth serum is a misnomer. They get talkative but they can still lie like a rug."

"Where did you get the C-117?"

"Out of my kit."

"That's some kit you have there."

"It serves my purposes. Master Sautto talked his head off. Not all of it is true, but a lot matches up with what you told me.

"When I got all that I was going to get, I drove back to the party area, parked the van along the street and picked up my car. Right now I'm heading back to Carmel. I just had to tell someone. I don't know what possessed me to make direct contact. I've never done anything like this."

Wanting to get more information and find out what Kahn's intentions were, Usher said, "That was a gutsy thing to do. How come you're headed back to Carmel?"

"It's going to be some time before Sautto can pull himself together enough to get loose, get dressed and drive. I know where there is a roadside rest area. I'm going to pull in there for a few winks and then get something to eat. I'd like to be watching when he gets home. Oh, yes, I disabled his cell phone so he can't call for help."

"Now that you have all of this information, what are you going to do with it?" asked Usher. "You don't dare turn it over to the authorities. They'd have you up for at least a half a dozen felony charges and judge daddy would probably see that they all stuck."

"Yeah, I know. I've been giving it some thought. You'll have to buy next week's "Orbiter." Oh, yeah, the murder weapon was there. It's part of something else. There are two round roller balls mounted on a shaft. A twelve-inch long square rod is attached to the cross bar. My battery is about dead and I need to get to the rest stop. See you." The phone went dead.

The coffee was ready to pour. Usher pulled a couple of mugs off the tree.

"My, you really started something," said Anasette.

"I hope Kahn can devise some way of keeping Sautto off the Supreme Court. Confirmation hearings can't be far away.

"I wonder what young Sautto will do once he wakes up. As soon as he can think straight, he'll realize someone knows he's the ball bearing rapist. And he'll have no idea what he may have said under the influence of that drug. He may not realize that he was injected with another drug."

"My hope is," said Anasette, "that Kahn's dirty little mind will come up with some way of getting that Sautto slime ball off the streets."

Usher gave a rueful laugh. "I probably made a good choice to find someone to do a nasty job."

CHAPTER 13

Anasette braved the cold to be on hand when "The Orbiter" hit the stand at her usual source. She was dying of curiosity. Kahn had not called back with any follow-up report. There had been nothing of interest on the national news. She had even dipped into the online newspapers from California. There was nothing.

Usher heard the van return to the garage. The elevator was on the ground floor. When it started up, he poured fresh coffee. There was no sedate entry as Anasette burst around the corner.

"At first I couldn't find it! Kahn has a long article, but nothing on Sautto. There are three black pages with white printing by a guest writer. It's entitled, 'Let Me Tell You a Story'. It starts out, 'Once upon a time'. Anasette shoved the open magazine under Usher's nose as she bounced onto her stool.

It was a long story concerning a depraved youngster who was always getting into serious trouble and a powerful father who continually bailed him out. There was no direct reference that would lead the reader to the Sauttos without inside information. However, if anyone was "in the know," then everything fit with great precision.

Anasette could hardly wait until Usher finished. "Did you note the supreme effort and court trouble? When you know the situation, the whole story is loaded with double and triple entendres. I wonder what Kahn is doing with the story."

"This is well done. If the Sauttos' associates read this, they'd probably never make the connection."

"There is also a Mexican drug cartel reference," pointed out Anasette.

"Those drug lords might not take too kindly to that kind of publicity."

An hour after Anasette had brought the papers back, the phone rang.

"Hey Kahn, a brilliant article." said Usher into the speakerphone.

"Yeah. I thought so myself. It shouldn't be too long until we see if there will be any results. A while ago I had hardcopies delivered to papa's DC hotel. The young Sautto is in Matamoros, Mexico, so I sent an email. Another copy has been stuck in the door at the Sautto house. The papers are open to my story.

"What do you think will happen?" said Usher.

"As far as pop is concerned, it all depends on how much guilty knowledge he has. I have a hunch he has quite a bit, from what his kid said.

"Oh yes, I sent e-mail copies to a couple of the cartel members who are over Sautto. In the story, I swapped first and last names and made acronyms. Few people would recognize them, but I bet the drug lords will recognize themselves."

"What happened when young Sautto got home?"

Kahn burst out laughing. "He didn't get back until mid afternoon. He looked like a dog had buried him and he hadn't been able to crawl out the hole. He'd been sick in that van. He got sick trying to clean it up. He still wasn't too steady on his feet. I was wondering how he was able to drive home.

"He cleaned himself up, raided his parent's house for two sacks of stuff. He threw those along with a suitcase into the BMW and headed for Mexico."

"What do you think will happen when the cartels figure out your article?"

"They were ready to put a bullet in my brain just on the suspicion that I might be going to look into their interests. I imagine they will give him the same unin¹formed consideration when it comes to Rufino's trustworthiness.

"Anyway, stay tuned to the news. Oh, Orlop, I know about you trying to grab that baby, but no one will ever hear about it through me. See you." Khan broke the connection.

Anasette said, "Kahn says, 'Watch the news.'" She dropped off her stool and headed for the TV set in the bedroom.

"Tomato?" said Usher.

"Sure."

Usher produced two very large, lush tomatoes from the basket. He cut them into halves, cored them and put each into a rice bowl. He added large dollops of cream cheese spread to each before depositing them in the microwave.

Anasette had adjusted the sound so they could keep track of the cable channel from the kitchen.

After eight minutes, the microwave went off. Usher served the tomatoes along with soup spoons.

"The only trouble I have with these is that I invariably fricassee my lip trying to eat them too soon."

Both jumped when the anchor said.... "Judge Sautto has suddenly, without explanation, canceled all of his appointments with the Senators, whom he had been appealing to for support in his confirmation hearing. He and his wife were reportedly flying back to California. The only comment was that it was for personal reasons. This is a developing story. We'll let you know as soon as something comes into the newsroom."

"That didn't take very long," observed Anasette.

"Kahn said, whatever happened depended on the degree of guilty knowledge. From this, I think we can infer considerable guilty knowledge."

The artists returned to the dining bar. "Yum," said Anasette. "This time I won't burn my lip."

After breakfast, Usher went to work surfing around the TV channels. The entire news community was frantically trying to find the reason for Sautto's sudden suspension of operations.

It was getting late enough to call Jangala. When the call got through, Usher said, "How's the Nyla deal coming along?"

"I think everything is in order."

Usher said, "It might be wise to bounce whoever you can to speed things up."

"What reason do you have to suggest that?"

That question didn't have the fire behind it that he had expected. It sounded more like a passing curiosity query. Jangala had always taken over the decision-making elements of all activities.

Pushing his wonderment aside for the moment, he asked, "Have you watched any TV this morning?"

"The morning news."

"What was the lead story?"

"The Supreme Court appointee."

"He broke off his interviews because he just found out that someone he didn't control knows that his son is the date rape father of Nyla."

That brought a more familiar reaction.

"What?"

"You're probably one of less than a dozen people who know that. Have someone go out to buy today's edition of "The Orbiter." You have the key to the story on the black pages. I'll talk with you after you've had a chance to read it." Usher broke the connection.

He didn't want to have to relate the story to the old man, because their original meeting was all too similar to the Sautto saga.

Jangala would be unhappy about being cut off, but Usher hoped that he would understand after reading the article.

Usher went back to the TV, expecting a call in an hour....plus or minus. He invited Anasette up for sandwiches for lunch. The hour passed. Anasette returned to her studio.

Usher flipped through the news channels. The tenor of the reporting changed. The anchors seem to be holding something that they didn't dare report. There were also indications that the newshounds were trying to locate Sautto family members to find any crisis that may have caused the interruption.

At martini time, Anasette came up in a fresh white bathrobe and clean wool socks.

"Has Jangala called yet?"

"No."

"Maybe he's paying you back for hanging up on him."

"Maybe and maybe a dozen different reasons. He...." Usher nearly toppled off his stool, trying to get to the TV set in the bedroom. A few moments later, Usher yelled, "Bring the martinis and come watch this."

When Anasette made it to the TV there were commercials.

"I heard Rufino's named. That was what attracted my attention. It must've been a tease for something after the break."

When the anchor reappeared, he started the segment with, "We are trying to confirm a report that the Supreme Court appointee, Judge Manuel Sautto's son Rufino, age 20, has been found dead in his Hermosillo condo. The death of the son couldn't have been the reason for the judge's early departure from Washington . The body hadn't been found yet." The report degenerated into time-consuming wild speculation.

"Kahn took care of Alecia's killer," said Anasette. "I don't know how I feel about that. I'm grateful Sautto didn't get away with that killing, which he probably would have if the authorities had tried to handle it. Pop and the liberal establishment would have intervened

"Now it looks like a cartel job. Those other date rapes will probably never be brought to light."

"Maybe someone will pick up on Kahn's story and actually put the pieces together."

As Usher was refreshing the martinis, Jangala's call came in.

"Orlop, you really know how to stir things up. Since your abrupt call suggested a little pressure, I've been pushing. Can you and Anasette bring our new mother and father to my house as close to mid afternoon tomorrow as possible? Nyla has just been released into my custody and she is already out of sight.

Tomorrow a nurse will bring her here and then depart. I don't want anyone to know the baby's destination. Will you arrange that?"

"Yes, I...." Click

Anasette went into a giggling fit. It started out with Jangala getting back at Usher but it quickly changed into glee that Maruca and Juan would get the baby they so deeply wanted.

Usher didn't even ask Maruca. He booked seats for four that would get them into Portland around 2:00 pm.

Then he called Maruca telling her what time she and Juan should meet him and Anasette at the ticket window. "We're going to pick up your baby. Pack for a couple of days."

Anasette was listening on the speakerphone. "She didn't hear anything beyond the word 'baby'."

Squeals and screams and babbled Spanish poured out over the speaker. Usher and Anasette sat back and enjoyed the sounds of joy.

Finally, Juan took the phone away from his celebrating wife. "Señor Usher, ¿Exactamente?"

"Exactamente, Juan." Usher repeated the time and told him to pack for a couple of days. "See you tomorrow."

The next 24 hours was an exhausting but satisfying journey. The foursome was picked up at the airport by a limo service.

Jangala had explained that he had maintained a sedan and a driver for many years. However, as his mobility deteriorated, he seldom left the house. A car and driver became an unneeded household extravagance.

Mrs. Kalunki seated everyone in the parlor before going for the boss. Jangala had opted for a wheelchair.

As Jangala situated himself across from the guests, Usher took over the introduction duties. He first presented Anasette. Of course they already knew each other via the phone. And then Usher presented the excited new parents.

As soon as the introductions were over and before any strained, inane conversation could develop, Jangala raised his hand and Mrs. Kalunki entered carrying a pink bundle. She walked straight to Maruca, who stood to take the baby.

Juan also stood to see the little face nestled in the blanket. Maruca was crying. Juan put a comforting arm around his wife.

Nyla had been sleeping, but with the transfer, she awakened and demonstrated the lusty lung capacity that Usher had noted at her birth.

Jangala spoke over the racket. "Mrs. Kalunki will show you to your rooms. Dinner will be at 6:00. One of the girls will take care of Nyla while you're dining."

The house domo led the new family away.

Usher noticed that the old man must have increased household staff. He could hear activities all around the house.

"Usher, would you push me into the office? We'll take coffee there. Anasette, walk with me."

Anasette walked alongside as Usher pushed.

"I've been looking forward to meeting you. Lyyli and Tanner are here frequently and seldom does a visit go by without reference being made to you."

When the trio reached the office, Usher deposited Jangala behind his desk. The old man levered himself from the wheelchair into his swivel chair as he continued to chat with Anasette.

Jangala waved a hand at the coffee service sitting on the open bar. "Would you pour me a rye, too?" Usher moved to comply with a smile on his face. Anasette was doing it again.

While he was at the bar, he poured a couple of martinis. When he served the coffee and the drinks, he placed Anasette's next to one of the armchairs in front of the desk, causing her to abandon her perch on the wheelchair.

Jangala swung around to face his desk and reassert his leadership of the occasion. "I think you have found a good set of parents for little Nyla. She deserves better than she has had so far."

"Maruca," said Anasette, "is one of the wonderful people the world. When we're down for some reason, we head for Dos Amigos. We went there the night Usher had to tell the authorities where to find that runaway once we knew he was wanted for a double murder. Maruca made our world right by the end of dinner."

"Tell me about the Dos Amigos," said Jangala.

Usher smiled, "One time I had to interview Maruca's former pimp, who in a weak moment gave a young fellow named Juan, Maruca's services at a discount. During the engagement Juan told his companion that he was saving to open a taco stand. Maruca gave him hell for buying her services when he should be saving for his stand.

"As time went by, Maruca helped Juan to open a stand. The zoning department or the health department kept closing down their operations for a violation of various regulations.

"Finally, they rented a house in a Mexican district and operated a carnita handout window from the kitchen. They made enough money and built a large enough following to open a regular restaurant. They changed locations a couple of times. Now Dos Amigos is where you go to get the best Mexican food. It's nothing lavish but it's clean, good, abundant and reasonable....and busy. Juan cooks and Maruca charms their customers."

Usher said, "I was rather surprised that it didn't take a harder sell to get your approval for a former Mexican prostitute. It has been my experience that you engage in your own rather stringent vetting process."

A rather crafty looking smile spread across Jangala's cratered face. "I did my work earlier. You were the focus of my work in those prior meetings. When I came to the conclusion that you could handle the matter, my work was done."

Anasette snickered and wagged her mane of black hair from side to side adding to Usher's discomfort.

Jangala continued. "Also Tanner and Lyyli have spent a considerable amount of time here. It is surprising how often the names of Usher and Anasette arise. In listening to them and their stories, I find you to have a rather far-flung family.

"Just last night, I called a charming lady and we talked for hours. Grandma V sends her love."

This time, a squeal of delight erupted from Anasette. "How are the girls?"

"They are blooming and the lights of her life." Jangala shoved his tumbler across the desk. "Please."

As Usher moved to comply, Jangala said, "Perhaps we should conduct a little business." Usher enthusiastically nodded his agreement, since he was never comfortable being the subject up for discussion.

"I have accommodations for you and Anasette and Maruca and Juan here. I also have an old-fashioned Finnish mama coming in to help the new parents weather their first night with an infant.

"In the morning, we are going to be joined by Tanner and Lyyli. They are anxious to see Nyla and her new parents. They want to visit with you, too. After breakfast, the attorney will be here to tie up all of the legal ends.

"In the afternoon, a Gulfstream will take you back to Denver. The family will be on its own. Have I missed anything?"

"Nothing, as far as I can see," said Usher. "However, another thought has come to mind." Both Jangala and Anasette wore expectant expressions. After a dramatic pause, Usher said, "Yes, we have developed a rather interesting extended family. We have just added two new members."

Anasette said "Nyla and....?"

"Mr. Jangala, of course. He rates the patriarch role."

"Of course," said Anasette with feeling. "I know several kids that would be living substantially different lives without his intervention. I wholeheartedly agree."

It had always been hard to read Jangala's moods, but on this occasion he seemed pleased.

CHAPTER 14

It wasn't even light yet when a discrete knock on the door sounded. Anasette nudged Usher to awaken him. By the second knock Usher was able to say,

"Yes?"

A female voice said, "Mr. Jangala needs Usher to come to the office right away."

"Coming," said Usher as all thoughts of sleep vanished and he swung his feet to the floor. "Something's gone wrong."

It didn't take long for Usher to pull a polo shirt over his head, get into a pair of pants and stuff his feet into shoes.

"I hope it has nothing to do with Nyla," said Anasette as she slipped out of bed to dress. She knew she couldn't compete with Usher on dressing speed, so she set off at her own pace.

Usher was out of the room while still buckling his belt. Jangala was behind his desk in a wheelchair. He was in his pajamas with a robe thrown over the top.

"Someone is trying to stop the transfer of guardianship. My

attorney's night answering service received a call from California that there would be papers filed in the morning to halt the transfer. My attorney called me before he headed for his office to try finding out what is happened. Do you have any idea what this could be?"

"There were a lot of couples trying to get a trophy baby. Maybe one of them has enough money to try buying the child. I doubt if the Sauttos have enough information to make such a move. I did hear the judge was able to postpone his confirmation bid for a month as a grief period. I'm just guessing. When can we find out what's going on?"

"Hämeenniemi was heading for the office as soon as he hung up." Jangala had seen Usher flinch when he heard that Finnish name that he would probably have to struggle with in the future. "If you ever have to call for Mr. Hämeenniemi, ask for Mr. Niko. Use Niko if you're talking to him.

"Back to business. He'll call as soon as he knows something. However, what do we do with our new parents?"

"Oh, boy," said Usher with feeling. "Unless the situation is rectified immediately, we'll have to say something. Juan can handle most anything, except maybe Maruca if something would take that baby away from her. Anasette should be here shortly. I'd like to hear her thoughts."

Further speculation was put on hold as Mrs. Kalunki brought in the coffee service.

Usher smiled at the older woman, who was up and running early, just like her boss. "Please put out another cup for Anasette. She should be along momentarily."

Anasette entered on cue, but not with her usual flare. Concern dictated her actions. "What's going on?"

"We had a tip that someone is trying stop the guardianship change," said Jangala. "That is all we know about it. My attorney is trying to find out more."

Anasette shifted her gaze to Usher. "Does Maruca know yet?"

"No. I hope we can get some clarification before she comes downstairs."

When the phone rang, Jangala checked the Caller ID and answered it himself.

"Hello, Mr. Hämeenniemi. What did you find out?"

Jangala proceeded to listen for a considerable length of time without an interruption. Finally, he said, "I'll call you within the hour with our instructions." Jangala hung up.

"I think we may be lucky. This all started by a couple of friends texting one another. The original message came from a forensics lab where a worker told her friend that there had been a match made on the father of Alecia's baby. The recipient of this message knew someone on Dr. McCann's staff. The word was passed on. The staff member called McCann, who hit the ceiling. He'd just given someone's baby away.

"My attorney had said that McCann was never completely comfortable with releasing the baby to what he saw as a very nebulous future. The dear doctor is now trying to get everything halted until the father can be identified. Apparently, there was a find in a database, but no one knows who it is at this point."

"How did you find out?" said Usher.

"McCann called my attorney's California representative trying to find the baby. He wanted to scoop up the baby and let the legal matters sort themselves out.

The doctor was very upset when he found the baby was no longer there."

"What's going to happen now?" said Anasette.

"It appears that the good doctor is going request the school file papers to revisit the case based on the discovery of new vital information."

"McCann is going through all this and he doesn't yet know who the father is," said Anasette, using a deprecatory tone.

"Don't be too hard on him. He's standing on a principle, not on a personality. Don't forget you know more about this case than he ever will." Turning his attention to Jangala, Usher said, "Do you think the school will do that?

"Probably. The school could be looking at a lawsuit for giving someone's baby to the wrong person. So could McCann since he was in charge.

"If this match comes from a database, then the police will be notified and the Sauttos will find out soon."

Jangala nodded agreement. "What do you think the Sauttos will do when they find out that they have a granddaughter floating around out there?"

"That's a hard one. My experience with Mexicans says that they are very family oriented. No matter what Rufino has done, he will always be their son and they would want his offspring. I don't know how they would react knowing the child was the product of a rape and the reason for a murder. However, Mexican feelings may be tempered to protect Manuel's position. Having a dead tourist son would probably not hurt his confirmation. Even an illegitimate granddaughter might not seem too bad. However, if you add serial rapist, murderer and cartel boss to the mix, everything changes."

"Soon I have to call my attorney. For the moment, I will have him not divulge anything and begin muscling up to defend the earlier action. I'm going to have him bring the papers over here at 10:00 am for signatures. None of the public papers have anything to do with Maruca and Juan. As soon as they sign their papers I want them to leave for Colorado and disappear. While I'm calling Hämeenniemi, you two go, get ready for the day and figure out what you're going to say to Maruca."

As Usher was shaving, Anasette said, "Maruca has always been strong and in control. That may not be the case on this subject, so don't get heavy handed."

"I can't bob and weave with Maruca. She'll see right through me. I'll have to be direct."

"What I mean is that you don't have to pose all the scenarios that are already crawling around in your skull."

"What about Juan?

"Maruca is his first concern. He'll do anything to protect her." Anasette thought for a moment before adding, "Including doing something foolish to protect Maruca's baby if he thinks that by doing so it will protect Maruca."

"Like what?

"Walking in the front door of their house and staying just long enough to pack a couple of bags before heading south to Mexico.

"Oh, boy."

A few minutes later, there was a bold knock on the door,

followed by a loud announcement....."Breakfast." The notice was repeated down the hall on Maruca and Juan's door.

So as to not meet in the hall, Usher and Anasette left immediately so that they were seated with Jangala when the new parents arrived. A radiant, smiling Maruca led the way into the dining room.

"How was the first night with a newborn?" said Anasette.

"Just as all mothers I've ever know have described it," said Maruca who was still riding a high.

Juan's countenance revealed more of the night's activities than his wife's.

After they were seated and had been served coffee, Usher said, "There has been a change in plans."

Maruca's smiles instantly changed to a look of slightly concerned anticipation.

"The attorney is bringing the papers over for signature at 10:00 this morning and then you, Juan, and Nyla are going to fly to Denver."

"Why? What has happened?"

"This morning Mr. Jangala received a tip that Nyla's father had been identified and that the doctor who was in charge is afraid he gave the baby to the wrong relative. There is a good chance that papers will be filed with the court to hold up any action until the father can be investigated."

As Usher spoke, Maruca's expression changed from concern into abject horror. In a flood of Spanish, Maruca jammed her chair back and fled for the second floor. Anasette started to follow, but she was stopped by Juan. "No Señorita, Maruca is my duty."

Turning to Usher he said, "What must be done?"

"Sign the papers, go to Denver and disappear into the barrio."

Juan quickly followed his wife upstairs.

"There is a good man," said Jangala. "The raw emotion that was displayed when Maruca realized what could happen reminded me of the face on my new sculpture."

"That would be one sculpture that I don't want to do," said

Usher.

Jangala rang the bell to have breakfast served. "Let's start thinking about what we have to do. Usher, you know the personalities down there the best. How are you going to proceed?"

Both Usher and Anasette picked up on the pronoun used.

"We don't have enough information to make any informed decisions. I may be able to find more if I can trace down Sasha Kahn. She should know as much as the doctor himself." When he got some raised eyebrows, he said, "Pillow talk. I don't have any numbers for her. I only called her in the hotel."

"Give me her name and address. I have a service that can find them. Then you can use the phone in your room to call her."

"I'll use my cell. She has Caller ID so she'll know it's me. We had a friendly relationship the last time I saw her and she probably won't connect me this directly with Nyla.

Further conversation was interrupted by Maruca and Juan reentering the room. Maruca was red eyed and puffy. However, she was carrying a wan smile.

"I'm terribly sorry I lost control of myself. All I could think of was that someone was going to take my baby. I just had to see her and make sure she was still here."

Juan seated his wife and took a chair himself. "Señor Usher, what are the new plans?"

Usher went over the sketchy information that they had on hand. "Once you finish here, Mr. Jangala will send you to an airport where a plane will take you to Denver. You'll have to figure out how to get home without leaving your name and address. Don't take a rental car or taxi."

"That is no problem. We can take the bus to a stop downtown and then have a friend or worker pick us up."

"From there on out, just go ahead with your life. If you attract any unwarranted interest by anyone, call me."

Jangala picked at his breakfast long enough to placate Mrs. Kalunki, before he escaped to his office. Shortly, the house domo returned with a slip of paper with Sasha's phone number. Usher also excused himself and headed for his room.

"Sasha, this is Usher Orlop, the sculptor from Denver."

"Hi, Usher. You don't have to remind me who you are. You are not one I'd likely forget. Are you back in California?"

"No. I was home for a little bit, but I'm out running around again. The reason I'm calling is that a little birdie tweeted in my ear that Baby A's father had been found in a date base and that Dr. McCann was going to try for a stay, or whatever the legal term is, in releasing Baby A to a new guardian."

"How in the world do you know that? None of that information has been made public."

"I had a little deeper interest in Alecia Arnold than I let on while I was in California."

"And you used me to pad that interest?"

"Your information was helpful in affirming that the plan was heading in the proper direction. Has Dr. McCann met with the board yet?"

"How do you know about that?"

"I need to talk to him before anything is done. Where is he now?"

"He's headed for Santa Jose. The meeting is at 2:00 pm."

"If your doctor brings this suit it could and probably will open up a chamber of horrors, which will adversely affect the lives of many people and the clinic. Can you find the doctor and set up a conference call between the three of us? I would suggest this be a private conversation with no extra ears or recorders because I will be giving you some information that could be dangerous. The police don't even know this. Two people are already dead, another one just missed death by a fraction and two more are trying to hide from death. There are probably more that I don't know about.

"You have my cell phone number. When you and the doctor are set up, give me a call. Get to phoning." Usher hung up.

Downstairs, the dining room table had been cleared so that four people could have a place to work. The attorney had just arrived and he was having a word with Jangala in the office. Maruca had run upstairs to check on Nyla. Juan was left to stand around looking nervous. Anasette was sightseeing. She was taking in all of the old objects d'art scattered around.

It wasn't until almost noon that Usher's cell phone rang.

"Usher, Dr. McCann and I are on a conference line. No introductions are necessary. You said you had something to tell us."

"Let me start off by saying that at this moment, Baby A is the most loved little girl on the planet. She is bringing great joy to a barren couple. She already has a fund set aside for her education and enough to launch her into the world. And she won't have to live life under the shadow of her birth.

"Now to other things. Doctor, do you know the identity of the father?

"No. That name has not been released yet. All we know is that a match has been made. In something this important, everything will be double checked before it is made public."

"I can tell you now, who the father is. His name is Rufino Sautto. Does that mean anything to you?

"No. Sasha?

"No."

"He is the son of Manuel Sautto." After an extended pause, Usher continued, "Judge Manuel Sautto."

"What?" demanded the doctor.

"Bristol?" said Sasha.

"The Supreme Court nominee. Without the DNA, how can you make such a statement?"

"Alecia Arnold was the victim of a serial date rapist. Alecia identified him and when she made contact, he killed her. Of course, none of this rape business will come to court. There is a report out that Rufino was found dead in his condo in Mexico. That story quickly disappeared. I don't really care one way or the other. Dead or alive, Rufino will never lay claim to Baby A.

"What you and the clinic have to be concerned with are the grandparents. Judge Sautto is rich enough and powerful enough to throw a lot of weight around. However, I plan on trying to talk him out of making any attempt to get Baby A. Educated self interest should dissuade him from making an attempt to change the current status quo. Should you open the game by putting a hold on the current plan, he might be enticed into entering the fray. Mexicans tend to take family matters rather seriously.

"I think you would be well served to delay any action until the lab confirms the Rufino Sautto is the father. The part involving Baby A is only a tiny part of a much larger, nastier game at play. You can get an inkling by finding a copy of last week's 'Orbiter'."

"Kalib. Is Kalib involved in this?"

Usher ignored the question. "Read the black pages. You won't understand most of it because you don't have to code words. If it is Kalib, he's on the right side for once."

"Kalib is never on the right side."

"Please, Sasha. Mr. Orlop, you are asking me to base my actions on a few unsubstantiated claims. I need to see that the clinic and all those connected with this unfortunate affair are protected."

"Then your best plan would to stay low. You and the clinic did what had to be done and now you are finished with the affair. You had no hand in placing Baby A, so you aren't involved there. Let the battle pass you by."

"You keep talking about a big fight. There is not going to be any big, bloody battle over placing a baby," said McCann.

"That's not the question. All of the dirt will come out if Manuel Sautto doesn't withdraw his name for consideration for the Supreme Court."

"Oh, boy. Politics."

"Any action you may be considering can be held in abeyance for a while, without jeopardizing your interests. I know there are others who must be consulted. After you have had your meeting I would appreciate a call letting me know what you are going to do. That will set up how I deal with the judge."

"I can do that. I have a meeting at 2:00. I have no idea how long it will be. Those guys have a tendency to nitpick."

After the call, Usher sat back to review the event. He had expected Dr. McCann to drag his heels more and to want more information. Of course, the doctor may plow ahead just as he had planned, ignoring the call. His one regret was that Sasha believed him to have used her as a source of inside information.

Usher was still sitting in the same chair when his phone rang.

Caller ID said it was Sasha again. "Hi Sasha."

"Usher, did you use me to further some political end? I would be very disappointed because I had pegged you as a nice guy."

"Sasha. It wasn't until after we had gone to Carmel that any of this came up. Your information was used to find a very good, loving home for a little girl that will provide for her into adulthood. Oh, yes. Please tell McCann that the new parents are aware of their daughter's situation and if anything looks abnormal, he will be advised. All the rest of this garbage came up after the father was identified through investigation."

"How does Kalib enter into this affair?"

"You'll have to ask him about that. I'm still not interested in the murder and all the rest of the stuff that is surfacing. I did what I wanted to do, but now I have to go back and try to preserve that work."

"I think Bristol is inclined to sit back and wait, but he doesn't know if the board will do so. I hope all of this is as you say. I didn't really expect to see you again, but you were a warm memory and I cherish warm memories."

After signing off, Usher went downstairs. The gathering in the dining room had broken up. Probably Maruca and Juan were getting ready to leave. Anasette was with Jangala in the office.

"How did you do with the doctor?" said Jangala.

"I think he will try to get the clinic to sit back and wait. I gave him the father's name, which they would get anyway as soon as the lab releases it. I told him this now had become a political matter. I suggested the clinic and the doctor would be wise not to become involved in politics.

"The thing that bothers me a bit is that Sasha thinks I may have been using her to further my own scheme. She called back after the conference call to ask me directly. I hope I convinced her that I hadn't misused her friendship."

"Where do you go now?" said Jangala.

"I need to talk to Judge Sautto, which might be a hard thing to do."

"That shouldn't be any problem for you. The first time we met, you bulldozed your way past Mrs. Kalunki to sit in that same chair you are now occupying when you were probably the last person on earth that I wanted to see at that time."

"Why don't you go say good-bye to Maruca and Juan," said Anasette, "and then go to the room to get a little privacy? A car will be here shortly to take them to the airport. I'll get them on their way and then come sit with Mr. Jangala."

Turning to Jangala, Usher asked, "Do you suppose that your network could locate where Sautto is right now and find a phone number where I can leave a note? Maybe I can leave a message to which he must respond."

"I should be able to come up with something."

"I'll also need another of those prepaid cell phones. I can't use my old one because it has your number in its records. If I get the same brand and model, I'll have a charged battery so there will be no holdup."

For a couple of hours Usher moved the various elements of his problem around in his mind. One thing was very clear....he couldn't play fair. Too much power was aligned against him. He and maybe everyone associated with this escapade could be in danger.

A booming voice broke into Usher's realm of thought. Tanner and Lyyli had arrived for lunch. That burst of enthusiasm would have been when Anasette appeared. She could always get a rise out of him by throwing in a little dance step or two.

It was time to get washed up and join the folks. He would have lunch and then begin fishing for Judge Manuel Sautto. He thought he had a choice enough chunk of bait to warrant a strike.

Usher walked into Jangala's office to join a high energy group with many new stories to tell. Jangala was content to listen. When lunch was called, the conversation flowed down the hall and regrouped in the dining room. Coffee was served back in the office. The conversation rolled on until Anasette spotted that they were losing Usher. She caught Jangala's eye and nodded toward the sculptor.

Jangala took over control of the group. "Usher, I forgot to tell you that as far as anyone knows, the judge is at his Carmel home. This is his home phone number. Here is the cell phone you ordered. Go take care of your duties."

"I don't want this call to come from here. I need to go to a Starbucks. I may have to wait for a while. I'll take a taxi back."

"When you're ready see Mrs. Kalunki."

Half an hour later, Usher had a fresh cup of coffee in hand and a seat in a secluded corner of Starbucks from which he dialed the judge's number. As expected he was picked up by an answering service.

"Judge Sautto, please return this call so I can give you a preview of your future should you not withdraw your name for consideration for the Supreme Court. I will elaborate on three subjects....rape, murder and cartels. I will stay by this phone for two hours. If I don't hear from you I will begin my blogosphere campaign to see you are rejected. The internet will love what I have to offer."

Usher broke the connection and leaned back to review what he would say on the return call....if it came in at all. As he rolled his head back to limber his tense muscles he found himself looking at the bottom of a surveillance camera. A whole new set of possibilities came cascading down on his mind. A federal judge is powerful person. Was he powerful enough to force the cell phone company to quickly trace his call and give a point of origin? Also, a judge might have the power to have local law enforcement try to locate the caller.

Usher hadn't foreseen such possibilities. Now he needed to work himself out of the problems of his own making. First he wanted to get out of the view of the interior cameras.

Casually Usher stood up, picked up his cup of coffee and headed for the side door to the parking lot. He didn't want to walk straight at the camera over the front door. Outside he took a drink of coffee and located two exterior cameras.

He didn't give either a decent view as he headed off into the parking lot of the big box home supply to the rear.

Usher stayed away from camera as he made his way to a park bench in a small part of the plaza dedicated to plantings. It was a warm enough day for him to spend the rest of the two hours outside, if necessary. From this vantage point he could see any unusual activity around Starbucks.

When his phone rang twenty minutes after placing the original call, Usher jumped, even though the ringer was muted. "Judge Sautto."

"Who are you and what do you want?" The growled question had a faint Hispanic accent.

"I'm just a conservative citizen who thinks your form of judicial radicalism doesn't belong on the Supreme Court. Now, with all the new baggage you're carrying I'm hoping to persuade you to withdraw."

"What's in it for you?

"Nothing, other than seeing justice is done, with as little collateral damage as possible. Everything about Rufino is going to come out, but it won't be as newsworthy if it can't be hung on a Supreme Court nominee...."

"What do you think you know about Rufino?" snarled the judge.

'Oh, I know he's the serial rapist....the Stainless Steel Ball Bearing Rapist. He's a murderer and I know he's high enough in the Cartels to have thugs at his disposal to kill others. The last I heard about Rufino was that he was found dead in his Mexican condo. However, that story has not been confirmed. It doesn't mean much whether he is dead or alive. Either way, he is the vehicle of your political demise."

"Ha," spit out Sautto. "None of that will ever be proven....at least not in time."

"Wait, Judge. None of this will be tried in your court. It will all be played out in the Court of Public Opinion. The internet and all those smart instrument users will love what we have to offer them. We have more info than the police."

Usher had to jerk the phone away from his head as Sautto erupted in his ear in loud and probably profane Spanish before severing the line of communication. There was a second click before the line went dead.

Usher smiled. He'd broken through the early arrogance that the judge had exhibited. He opened his own cell phone to call Mrs. Kalunki for a ride home.

Everyone was packed into Jangala's office waiting to hear his report. Anasette even had poured a cup of coffee to avoid any more delay than was absolutely necessary.

Usher took a drink of coffee and began his story by telling what he had left on the answering machine and then spending much of the time waiting for the return call trying to minimize his security video time and accuracy. "I even carried my coffee cup way off site so no one could find fingerprints or DNA.

"Since I'd built up that whole scenario about being found by GPS and the police catching me in Starbucks or identifying me through surveillance tapes, I was surprised to get a call back in twenty minutes."

Usher went through the call with the judge. When he was finished, Jangala said, "What was your thinking in making this approach?"

"My purpose was to prevent him or his wife from getting any thoughts of making an attempt to get their granddaughter. My idea was to give them enough to worry about so they won't be thinking about bloodlines."

"Do you think you succeeded?" asked Anasette.

"I think it will be like Kahn said, that it will depend on how much guilty knowledge pop had. If the old man has gotten the kid out of a rape charge before, he'll probably believe me. If this is new information, then he might ignore what I had to say, believing I'm just a conservative rabble-rouser. This is the chance of a lifetime for Sautto and it may be slipping away. He'll fight hard."

"Do you think the judge knows about the murder?"

"Rufino didn't seem to have anything else important enough to warrant the flight from Washington, so the chances seem good that pop came home to take care of Rufino's problems. Rufino could have called when Kahn was watching him stagger around. If he called when his mind was all messed up he could have told pop everything or the most convenient lie."

Jangala brought the speculation to an end. "What is you plan of action now or are you going to wait to see what he does?"

"As soon as I finish my coffee, I'm going to sic Kahn on him again. I hope Kahn hasn't gotten word that Rufino's DNA was identified in a databank. I want to drop that on him. That should really fire him up. I'll tell him about my call to Sautto, particularly since the dear judge found out he couldn't control the court action. The Court of Public Opinion is Kahn's court and he's a fancy stepper there. I'm also going to suggest he sees that this gets onto the internet to really set the judge off. I'd rather keep the pressure up and not just respond to Sautto's thrusts."

Neither Tanner nor Lyyli had entered into any of the discussions, since they were not a part of the operation.

Usher shoved his cup away and stood. "I'm going up to the room and try running Kahn down. I don't know how long that will take. I'll let you know what happens."

When Kahn picked up on the third ring, Usher figured that this number was the reporter's lifeline.

"What do you want Orlop?"

"Kahn, your phone-side manners need some work. Here I'm calling to give you some information and you make me want to hang up as if you'd answered with a rude expletive."

"Don't get huffy....that's just the way I am. Didn't mean nothin' by it. What do you have?"

"Received word that a DNA match was made on Baby A's blood. Papa was in a data base. My info doesn't identify papa, but you know I suspected Rufino. As of this morning, the police didn't have word of the match. They may have it now, but my understanding was that everything would have to be double checked before any release.

"Just a little while ago I talked by Judge Sautto."

"You what?"

"Yes, I called Sautto's home number and left a message he couldn't let go by. I received a call-back in twenty minutes." Usher told Kahn pretty much verbatim what was said.

Kahn laughed. He caught the court inference immediately. "What are you going to do next?"

"I have already done what I intended to do and that was to call you. Now that I have done that I'm going to get back to the studio and get some work done. Oh, one thought did occur to me. If that blue van is still in the garage at Sautto's, it might be fun to publicly try to purchase that rape-mobile, completely equipped with all the goodies such as light-tight curtains, date rape drugs, restraints, stainless steel ball bearings, murder weapon and such. You might even pull some more rape victims out of the bushes."

"Yeah. I'll put it in the pot, stir it around and see what happens." Kahn broke the connection.

Anytime Usher had to deal with Kahn, he had the feeling that a big mistake had been made. Usher clipped the phone on his belt and went down to deal with return tickets to Denver.

CHAPTER 15

Both Usher and Anasette were glad to be home, but the external anxieties continued to press down on them. There were still two days to wait for "The Orbiter." Both were anxious to find out what Kalib would do. They were both keeping abreast of the news for any word that Sautto was withdrawing his name from consideration. There were contrary rumors floating around that he was setting up a new schedule of appointments.

No one seemed certain as to why he had taken the time off. Originally, it was assumed it had to do with the death of his son, but that report remained unconfirmed and Sautto took no steps to deal with a death in the family. The only thing he would say was that his son was abroad.

A couple more days passed and there was still no sign that Sautto was withdrawing his name. Usher was beginning to fret.

Usher and Anasette were seated in the Great Room polishing off a bottle of wine from a former dinner before they headed for their respective beds. Anasette hadn't turned on the electric blanket when she arrived and Usher was in no mood to advance a proposition. Both artists were of a mind to hold their own councils. As Usher settled back after pouring, he said, "Does the name 'Frank Buck' mean anything to you?

Anasette swirled her wine in the glass for a bit before answering. "The name is familiar but I can't place it."

"We're too young to remember directly, but he was one of the early animal trappers and trainers. There was a book and then a movie, if I remember correctly, called 'Bring 'Em Back Alive'. In recent times 'Bring 'Em Back Alive' became the Twitter name for an outfit that advocates for exploited girls. To make the letter count for Twitter, it became bringmbackalive. Date rape is one of their main concerns. This organization has a lot Twitter followers. Every tweet they send out goes to nearly half a million people. Of course only a small percentage of them will see any given tweet."

"Where in the world did you come up with this information?" said Anasette.

"I was eavesdropping on the booth behind me one day. After I made the claim to Sautto that the internet would love my information, I've been worrying how to use the social networks in such a short time. I don't know that much about them. I spent a good part of the afternoon trying to find my way around all that stuff. Wow."

"I can't help you on any of that," said Anasette as she snuggled down further into her robe. "You're going to have to think of something. As far as I can see from my cruising around the news media, the only time Sautto's name comes up on any of the networks or major papers is to heap praise on senior. The rightwing talk shows have the judge in their gun sights."

"Yeah, I've noticed the same thing. I wish I know what Kahn was planning."

The next morning Usher called Sasha.

When Sasha answered the phone she sounded a little suspicious when she said, "Hi, Usher. What are you up to?"

"I've been wasting scads of time listening to news reports and scanning your local papers. From what I can see, the Sauttos have disappeared from the face of the earth except for gratuitous praise for papa. Do you know if the data bank has released the name of the father yet?"

There was a hesitation.

"Sasha. Let me tell you a story. Baby A has a new milk-name of 'Nyla'. As of now she has not exhibited any extraordinary conditions. Since she arrived in her new family, her mother has not been out of hearing range. Her glowing father is just as adept at taking care of a baby as anyone. The world in which she is now living is a happy one. Her parents are well thought of and admired in their community. Nyla has a running start on her future.

"This was my goal in this whole affair. I am hoping that it will remain the same."

"Thanks, I needed that," said Sasha. "The police have a name but they won't release it to the Clinic. They say they have an open investigation and they can't give us the name until their investigation is complete. Bristol has not told them that we have a name. At this point we don't know if the names match."

"Tomorrow, 'The Orbiter' comes out. I'm expecting another article."

"You didn't answer me the other day about Kalib's part in this."

"I danced around it because I know how you guys feel about one another. I don't want to have input into such a virulent feud. If he wishes to discuss any part he may have had in this affair, I'll let him do so. I might say that if he does wander by your wagon, don't throw him under the wheels until he has had a chance to say something.

"Thanks, Sasha. I still have some work to do."

Usher waited until he was sure Szedlak would be up and moving.

"What do you want Orlop?"

"Is that the way to greet a guy who is trying to find an outstanding member of the local constabulary who wants to add a few more arrest scalps to his belt?"

"What are you talking about?"

"I need someone to clear up some felony cases."

"What kind of cases?"

"If you must know, they're date rape cases."

"How many?"

"Three and maybe more. Boy, are you nosey. Drop by about lunch time and I'll see if I can womp up soup and a sandwich."

"I'm not on duty until 7:00."

"Good, then we won't be interrupted, and you can have a leisurely meal for once."

"See you at noon." Szedlak hung up.

Usher stomped on the floor above Anasette's apartment before calling her. When she answered, he said, "Kaz is coming over for soup and sandwich at noon. Can you make a run to the store while I get the bread going?"

As soon as Anasette had her list, Usher started on the bread, so that there would be enough time for it to rise. He probably shouldn't have been so ambitious and just gone to the bakery.

However, at noon Anasette was ladling the onion soup into bowls. Usher was stuffing slices of broiled chicken breast, topped with sprinkles of blue cheese, into a round, flat loaf of bread that had been sliced horizontally like a bagel. The loaf was then cut into six pie-slice shaped sandwiches. Szedlak was urging haste.

As the sharpness of appetite was blunted, Szedlak said, "What's this rape business you were talking about?"

Anasette made a face. "Please, wait until we finish eating."

"Sorry," said the lieutenant. Since he couldn't talk, he would eat. He shoved his bowl to Usher for more soup as he eyed the second part of Usher's sandwich.

In case Anasette's enormous appetite hadn't been satiated yet, the sculptor cut the remaining wedge in half and offered it to the big eaters.

After the dishes were cleared and the coffee served, Usher got down to business and explained the date rape suspicions he had for Rufino in Alecia's case. "An associate was doing some internet investigation and came across two other reported rapes involving a stainless steel ball bearing in the same area. There could be more."

Szedlak scrunched his face up. "You're getting ahead of yourself. You have to have positive identification that will stand up in court before you can start piling other rape charges on. In fact, even if you get a positive DNA connection with your Ruffy guy and the dead girl, it still could have been consensual sex three-quarters of a year ago.

"Now we get down to the fun part. If you do establish your Ruffy is the father and that paternity was gained by rape, what is that squirrely little brain of yours going to do with it?" Szedlak chuckled. Anasette gave a giggly chirp.

"Actually," said Usher without a pause. "I just want to try out a new law enforcement procedure. Follow me."

Usher led the way into his end of the building. Szedlak had been up there after all the windows has been Uzzied out, but he'd never seem it in proper form. He was all eyes.

After pulling up a couple of side chairs to the computer, Usher woke up the Mac and called up his Twitter page. "I opened a Twitter account a while back, but I have never spent much time on it. I'm only following this number....285. That other number 191 is the people who are following me. When I tweet, which is what my message is called, it will reach those who follow me.... the 191. When any one of those I am following tweets, I get it on my screen. The tweets of the 285 I follow pass down my screen. See the number at the top of the column? While I'm working on the page, new tweets are held back until I release them or close out. Look at how quickly tweets stack up, and I am only capturing the output 285 out of the millions getting sent."

In a text box at the top, Usher entered "Hi Anasette." He hit the "tweet" box and the greeting dropped down to head the line of avatars.

"That just went out to all 191 of my followers. I only have 140 letters and spaces per tweet. You must be brief."

Usher could see that Szedlak was anything but impressed. Anasette was just looking at a new thing. "Watch this." Usher typed "bringmbackalive" into a box and hit enter. The pages changed. Little avatars lined up down the left side of the two column page.

Usher pointed at the top of the right page.

"Wow," said Anasette. There are over 12,000 following and nearly a half-million followers.

Usher put the computer back to sleep as he led the way back

to the coffee pot.

"Okay, I'm duly impressed with a half-million twitters. What do you want?" said Szedlak.

"I'd like to compose a good strong tweet asking girls who felt that they might have been date raped and found themselves in possession of an unexplained stainless steel ball bearing to click 'here,' which would open an email to the organization. I can't do it as a plain old citizen unless I make a case for that group, which I don't want to do. But a law enforcement agency could legitimately ask for assistance in finding a serial rapist."

"So you want me to front your idea?" said the lieutenant. "Hell, you don't even have a single positive match. For a fishing trip like that, you need something more than your hunch. I could never sell the department on anything like that."

"I see your point," said Usher. "What I'm more interested in is your thoughts about using Twitter to get a message out. A good percentage of those followers will be young women, and those young women talk among themselves. Another factor that could come into play is that someone who might call in doesn't have to take down a number or address or change to another form of communication. She just clicks and proceeds on."

"It may work out well, but first you have to have something to put out. Thanks for the lunch. I've got some business to conduct before offices close."

Szedlak let himself out. As the door was closing Anasette said, "You didn't get much mileage out of you soup and sandwich."

"Oh, I think I have enough. It takes a while for Kaz to get comfortable with new things. As he thinks about it, those numbers will become more impressive to him. My first problem is to get enough proof for him take another look at the procedure."

"Where do you go from here?"

"No sense in searching for new stuff, when known stuff is still available."

Anasette gave Usher her best squashed bug look.

"What? I'm going to call Kalib to see if he recorded the source of those two date rape cases he told me about. I'll ask if he found any more. I'll also inquire if he knows if the lab report is public yet. Then I'll call Sasha to see if she knows anything more. Should these sources prove to be uninformative, then I'll start new searches."

Usher spent the rest of the evening and far into the night laying out his plan of action and writing his presentation material.

By the time Szedlak was up, Usher was ready for him. When the phone was picked up, Usher hit the send button to pass a ton of email material over to the lieutenant. After the usual grumbled opening, Usher began his presentation. "That DNA information has been given to the police and the medical authorities, naming Rufino as the father of Baby A. So far, the public has not been notified. I would suspect that the judge can block the locals from putting out the word. It will have to come from some other source.

"I tracked down those other two stainless steel ball bearing reports and they are included in the email. I also threw in an inquiry I found about another similar case. There is geographic information concerning the rapist's known range."   Usher continued to enumerate all the material contained in the file.

Finally Szedlak interrupted. "You've already proven you're a good investigator. Where are you going with this?"

"View this as an experiment in the value of the new media in law enforcement problems. If you want to demonstrate your acumen in the new roll of law enforcement in the exploding digital age, you take this file to whoever handles such things in your department and ask for permission to engage in this experiment. I'll make the pitch to Frank Buck Rescue, the owners of the 'bringmbacalive' twitter account to send out tweets periodically for two days. In the end you will get a complete report on the responses to message. You can then direct positive responses to the appropriate departments. Denver PD can glow in the high praise for its charge into the future."

"Step out of that cow pie and tell me about the other side of the coin."

"There's not too much out there to go wrong. You're not doing anything but asking for assistance. If you were to find a case in your backyard through this and screw it up, then there could be some repercussions."

"What's in it for you...to do all this work?"

"A seventeen-year-old girl is dead and her little girl doesn't have a mother. The crud that started this off and probably killed her will get away free because his powerful father can protect him. Maybe enough furor can be drummed up so a little justice can slough over into this case. Don't forget you have a piece of this too. Those two Mexicans you have in jail were sent after me by that same crud."

When Usher hung up, he wished Szedlak would exhibit more enthusiasm. He had agreed to take the proposal to the person who was coordinating that type of activity. The chief hadn't set up any specific department for that. Usher tried to emphasize the need for haste without arousing any suspicions.

Now it was a waiting game. Another minor wait was just beginning. Anasette was just pulling out in the van to get the new edition of "The Orbiter." It would be a while, because Anasette would almost memorize all of Kalib's writings before bringing it back for him to see. That way she had a basis to question his thoughts without having to refer to the printed page.

Usher turned on the cable channels to see if Judge Sautto was on any type of move. He put on a new pot of coffee awaiting Anasette's return.

"He did it again," yelled Anasette as she exited the elevator. She bounded across the room and hopped onto her stool. She slapped the paper down in front of Usher before starting to strip off her outer layers.

"There are four more black pages. He's telling the same story but in a more expanded way using the same characters. It still would be hard for someone to follow without his decoder ring. Without knowing who it is for real, you begin to feel like that crowd is really evil."

Usher read the article through thoroughly before commenting. "Good, no one is going to recognize the ball bearing rapist from this. Did he write another article?"

"Yep. It was on a completely unrelated subject in another state. He was his normal nasty self. I wonder if he arranged for the same circulation."

"Not unless he wanted to add someone to the list. The old ones would probably be waiting to see who the delivery boy was. If they received a paper last week, they probably had runners out to pick up the new one just as you did."

"I've been watching, but only a few of the rightwing media outlets made any mention of the first article. It was ignored by the major media. I wonder if it will be the same on this one."

"Probably. This doesn't further the progressive agenda, so they ignore it. If they all pass on a story, it goes by unnoticed by the public in general, leaving a completely false sense of reality. I have to figure out how to get the Rufino story out in front."

CHAPTER 16

Suddenly, Usher was no longer having to sit on his hands waiting for something to happen. Szedlak called to grudgingly report that the communication guru had been fascinated by the possibility of gathering information through Twitter. He'd ordered Szedlak to see if a test could be implemented immediately. He wanted to have a news conference to display the new concept as soon as it was a reality.

It took a while to get to the proper level of authority in the Frank Buck Rescue group. Usher laid out his proposal, showing the benefits to the organization in free publicity, participating in a new concept and the socially redeeming possibility of actually doing some direct good. As soon as Usher had the proper person, he sent all the material in an email so that they both were looking at the same program.

The conversation ended by Usher providing the Frank Buck guy with the name of the Denver PD communication coordinator. To make sure a connection would be established, Usher called Szedlak with the Rescue guy's name and number.

Anasette came up for a martini, but she soon realized that Usher was in some other world. After a quick drink she retreated to her apartment and left him to get on with the current interest.

For his part, Usher absently found enough bits and pieces in the refrigerator to keep his hunger at bay while he pondered his next step. His success probably rested on the showing on Twitter. That was his best chance of success and if the opening presented itself, he had to be ready to strike at that moment. So he started the next phase.

From the two issues of "The Orbiter," Usher copied each of the black pages. He enlarged and printed each page onto a letter-sized format. Then, with a white pencil, he changed the names and various other identifying marks to properly identify the various participants. He made sense of all the acronyms that Kahn had used. The final effort brought in the Stainless Steel Ball Rape cases and firmly associated them with Rufino Sautto, son of Judge Manuel Sautto.

Before going to bed he scanned the altered pages and made them into a PDF file ready for transmission.

Despite the short night, Usher was up early to check the various news reports. When he heard the water running long enough to swish out the coffee pot and fill it, Usher stomped the floor and called down. "The coffee is already made up here."

"I'll be right up." Right up always allowed for a quick shower and a brushing of the teeth.

Usher's greeting was, "You were still working when I got up in the middle of the night." She left her statement dangling there waiting for an explanation.

"Oh, I got busy."

"Beast!" Anasette took a couple of quick steps to get closer before executing a theatrical stomp near Usher's toes.

Usher feigned an exaggerated defensive move as if that tiny sock-covered foot could have done damage.

Both had a little laugh before Anasette hopped up on her stool, accepted a cup of coffee and said, "What's up?"

"I could use a little help today monitoring the media."

"What are you looking for?"

"A number of things. I arranged for a series of tweets through bringmbackalive.com concerning the Stainless Steel rapist. The communications officer here was enthusiastic, as was the guy at Frank Buck. I want to know if this new use of the social media was noted and by whom. Also I want the latest on the activities of the judge, and finally I'm interested in any info concerning Rufino. Will you surf through the channels today and note anything on those items? I'll be doing the same up here. At martini time we can compare notes."

It proved to be a long day. Usher couldn't do much while he channel surfed the major news media. He was able to browse most of the major newspapers while he waited for the TV news to recycle. It wasn't until noon break that something positive happened. One of the news channels mentioned that a new social media experiment apparently had located two more victims of a serial rapist. By the 1:00 o'clock news it was a hot item.

The only comments pertaining to the judge were about his rescheduling of his Senate visits. Rufino was still among the missing.

As bedtime neared, Anasette clicked on the electric blanket. Before she returned to her seat in front of the TV, Usher said, "Hand me the cell phone. Let's see if Kahn is still up. I have something to send him."

Anasette didn't have an opportunity to question Usher before he dialed.

"What do you want Orlop?"

"Aren't we in a fine mood this evening? I was calling to congratulate you on a fine follow up article and you growl at me."

"You'll thank me and then still want something."

"Since you brought it up, are you where you can receive an email?

"Yeah."

As Kahn recited an address, Usher entered it in his computer and hit the send button "This file has copies of each of your black pages. I have made a multiple choice code key, which you might find interesting. All the correct names are included. A little bit of investigating will reveal the correct ones. You are free to reject it, alter it, or use it. Since the mainstream media has jumped on the twitter story, this will hook your story and the twitter story together. The media can't as easily drop it. It's your call....let me know."

After the call to Kahn, Usher was still dissatisfied with the state of things. "It's as if I just finished dinner and I'm not satisfied. I ate enough, but I want something more."

"I know that feeling well. I call it a 'chocolate craving'," said Anasette with a smile. "That reminds me. You haven't been by that nice little bakery in ages."

"I must be slowing down. I haven't been in the dog house for quite some time," said Usher with a loud sigh.

Usher thought for a bit. "If by 10:00 am we don't hear of Sautto withdrawing, we'll take a little drive away from here so I can call Sautto. After that call, we'll pass by the bakery and I'll buy two of those chocolate things."

"Four. You're going to want me to monitor the TV for a couple of days."

"Okay, four."

Chapter 17

Sautto made no changes, so at 10:00 am Usher backed his classic car out of the studio. While waiting for the garage door to close, he revved up the engine to get that satisfying Mustang cackle, which brought a smile to his face. Anasette didn't enjoy the racket but she smiled at the enjoyment her friend received from the action.

It was a beautiful winter day. The world was sparkling as the sunlight bounced off the snowy surfaces. Since the car heater was pulling yeoman duty, even Anasette appreciated the foray.

The pair ended up on top of Lookout Mountain, a high lookout point out toward Golden. The view was spectacular. After doing justice to nature, Usher pulled out his Sautto cell phone and dialed the Judge's home number. When the answering service picked up the call, Usher said, "Morning, Judge. You know who this is. I'm calling to see what you thought of our opening arguments in the Court of Public Opinion. Those "bringmbackalive" tweets brought in a couple more possible stainless steel ball bearing rape cases and the mainstream media guys jumped all over it. Point number two of my opening argument is to supply the media with Rufino's name.....”

“Pinche Cabrone, who do you think you are?” roared the judge.

In the background came a plaintive call, “Rico.”

“Callate, Bruja.? (Shutup, witch)

Usher injected a sharp, “Aha,” into the phone before dropping into a soft, sibilant tone. “So you are the cartel jefe, ‘Rico’, who sends young toughs out to kill people. Boy, will I have fun with this.”

The phone was slammed down hard. The first time, the hand set missed the cradle.

Usher sat back with a smile on his face.

Anasette had been able to hear everything even without the speaker phone, “What do you think he'll do now?”

“He'll move now. He has to start building his own defense.” Usher started the Mustang and left its signature echoing through the canyons and over the plains. He headed for the bakery.

THE SUMMATION

It wasn't until the next morning that things began to move. The media was going crazy trying to get specific information. Sautto had again cancelled his interviews with the Senators. All that the judge's people would say was that the judge will make a formal statement later in the day. No hints were given as to what the statement would cover. No time was given for the promised statement.

Finally, the word came out that a spokesman would read a statement from the courthouse steps at 4:00 pm. Anasette came up to watch the event, which was woefully short. It was carried live on national TV. The judge wrote that the Mexican government had just given him positive identification that a body recovered at Mazatlan was indeed that of his missing son, Rufino. The judge and his family were leaving immediately for Mexico to deal with this tragedy. After that he planned to retire to his ranch in Mexico. Therefore, he was withdrawing his name for consideration for the Supreme Court. After that, he thanked those who had backed him for the high court.

Usher was energized. "Let's go to Dos Amigos for dinner. I think we can tell everyone to relax and breathe now."

When they walked in, Maruca was not in evidence. Usher asked a server, "Is Maruca around?"

"Oh, yes, she's in the baby room." She motioned to the right rear corner.

Before they got there, Usher started laughing. The big round booth that had been in the corner had been moved down near the kitchen door. In its place was a new fenced in playpen. In the kitchen wall of the pen was a new Dutch door. Through the open upper half they could see Maruca burping Nyla. Maruca shooshed the approaching artists as she transferred the drowsy baby into her basket.

Maruca turned down the lights and left the door ajar before hugging both Usher and Anasette.

"Juan and I are so incredibly happy, it's hard to believe we are not just dreaming."

"You bring her to work with you?" said Anasette.

"We have a business to run and I could never turn Nyla over to a babysitter all day and half the night. We just took a little space from the storeroom and a little bit from the kitchen so Nyla has her own room and I can tend her whenever it's needed. Actually she has three mothers most of the time. When the girls are finished with their work, you can find them in playing with the baby. Juan has a baby monitor in his kitchen."

"Isn't the playpen stocked with toys a little advanced for Nyla?" said Usher.

"We made that for the future, but we found it was good for business. My customers dump their kids in there while they sit back and enjoy another cerveza."

Juan stuck his head out of the kitchen to say hello and reported that the Huachinango was particularly fresh and good.

Later, as Usher and Anasette were sipping Presidente Brandy from their coffee cups, Usher asked if Juan could join them for a few minutes.

When Juan slid into the booth, Usher said," I'm going to call Jangala and give him some information. I thought all of you would find it of interest."

Usher set his new cell speakerphone on the table and dialed Portland. "Mr. Jangala, Usher here. Anasette and I just finished a marvelous dinner of Huachinango....Snapper. Maruca and Juan are here listening."

"Good evening Maruca, Juan," said Mr. Jangala. "How are you finding parenthood?"

"Oh, Señor Jangala, Juan and I are so happy. Anything is worth this happiness. Thank you, thank you, Señor."

"Wonderful. Cherish each moment because it will be quickly gone."

"Sir," said Usher. "You should see Dos Amigos. Part of the back corner has been remodeled into an area for a playpen outside of a Dutch door into Nyla's room. There is always a willing attendant within a half dozen steps.

"Before someone comes and drags Juan away, I want to pass along some information. If everyone has been watching you will know that Judge Manuel Sautto is packing his bag to go bury his son, who was probably killed by a cartel hoodlum preying on tourists. Then he's going into retirement in Matamoros, Mexico.Therefore, he is reluctantly foregoing further service to the country by declining an appointment to the Supreme Court.

"What he is not saying is that his son had been identified as the Stainless Steel Sign rapist. It came through a database, which the judge was apparently blocking. But the word was spread by "The Orbiter" and the internet, which the judge could not control. The Court of Public Opinion was informed and eventually they would reach a verdict that the judge could not block.

"Another little item that only us five now know is that while Sautto was railing at me on the phone, a woman I took to be his wife called him 'Rico'," which was the name of the cartel jefe that ordered those two young thugs to kill Kahn and attack Anasette and me. When I bounced him with that jefe observation, he slammed the phone down and apparently began his move.

"A little earlier this afternoon I picked up a message on my answering machine from Kalib Khan, who said, "For the final chapter in the Rufino Sautto escapades go to such and such an internet address.

"The site is a Mexican wire service, which reports that a body was found in the surf at Mazatlan. It was believed to be that of an American tourist whose name is being withheld at this time. The cause of death was a small caliber bullet to the base of skull leading authorities to believe it was a cartel killing.

"If that is Sautto, as Kahn indicates," said Usher, "then the earlier rumors about him being killed in his own condo were wrong. I wondered what had happened to that story."

"He may have been killed in the condo," said Jangala. "That site or those circumstances might have been inconvenient or a story hard to handle for either the judge or the Mexican government....or both. The random shooting of a tourist in a resort town is easier to pass off than the murder of a politically potent figure in his house. I doubt if we'll really know for sure."

"Good riddance, in any case," said Anasette with feeling.

"Did you notice," said Usher, "how the mainstream media pounced all over that innovative way of locating that sex offender? They really chomped onto that story and then when the ball bearing rapist was identified as Rufino, they couldn't back out of such as splendid story. Now they are going to have to deal with the judge's kid. They can't shove it under the rug. That should generate some national coverage.

"In any case," said Usher, "I think we can now relax. However, it happened, Rufino is not around to make any paternal claim. There is so much dirty laundry laying around out there that it would seem unlikely that any governmental board would look favorably on any Manuel Sautto claim on a granddaughter especially now after she was the product of a rape and later brutal murder by his son.

"And then there is the Cartel connection. When those two toughs at the Denver jail gave me the name 'Rico,' I thought they were referring to Rufino. It didn't even dawn on me that it could be a Superior Court Judge."

"What do you plan to do now?" said Jangala.

"The only thing I see that needs to be done is to call Sasha and thank her for her help and encourage her to see that Dr. McCann and the medical facility don't screw things up."

Suddenly there was a full throated squall coming from the

nursery. Instantly Maruca was in mother mode. Juan was in backup position even with the two food orders a waitress had just handed him. Moments later, Usher and Anasette were alone, with Anasette giving Jangala a blow-by-blow description of the happenings and local color.

As things wound down, Usher said, "We'll sign off now and I'll send you some photos. This new phone has a camera."

"Thank you. Goodnight."

"Goodnight, Yrlo," said Anasette sweetly as Usher rolled his eyes.

ISBN 978-9847524-0-9